"It was the end of summer, a hot night when all of Darlinghurst goes in search of a party. The humidity gets under the skin and creates a sexual friction, and before you know it the streets are crawling with people in search of some kind of contact—the brush of fingertips, a kiss, anything. I was in huntress mode, adorned to swallow some man up. Dressed in a blue skintight number, stretched tightly across my breasts and pulled down to expose my shoulders, I felt hot. Let's face it, I *was* hot, my vows of celibacy evaporating every time my garter belt rubbed against my thighs."

—from "Man of Sighs," in *Quiver*

TOBSHA LEARNER was born in the United Kingdom and has lived there, the United States, and Australia. She has worked extensively for stage, television, radio and film. Among her plays are *Glass Mermaid, Wolf, SNAG,* and *Seven Acts of Love as Witnessed by a Cat..* Her novel *Madonna Mars* will be published in 1998. *Quiver* is her first collection of short stories.

QUIVER

A BOOK OF
EROTIC TALES

Tobsha Learner

A PLUME BOOK

PLUME
Published by the Penguin Group
Penguin Putnam Inc., 375 Hudson Street, New York,
New York 10014, U.S.A.
Penguin Books Ltd, 27 Wrights Lane, London W8 5TZ, England
Penguin Books Australia Ltd, Ringwood, Victoria, Australia
Penguin Books Canada Ltd, 10 Alcorn Avenue, Toronto, Ontario,
Canada M4V 3B2
Penguin Books (N.Z.) Ltd, 182–190 Wairau Road, Auckland 10,
New Zealand

Penguin Books Ltd, Registered Offices:
Harmondsworth, Middlesex, England

Published by Plume, an imprint of Dutton NAL,
a member of Penguin Putnam Inc. First published by
Penguin Books Australia Ltd.

First Plume Printing, July, 1998
10 9 8 7 6 5 4 3

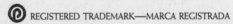
CIP data is available.
ISBN 0-452-27984-4

Printed in the United States of America

The Koi San are the hunters and gatherers of the Southern African savannah. They are known to hunt with arrows and have a respect for their prey that borders on the mystical. Besides their hunting pouch, they also have a smaller, magical quiver filled with tiny love arrows. These are kept for the women they desire.

CONTENTS

THE WOMAN WHO WAS
TIED UP AND FORGOTTEN

Sandra and Brian are a middle-aged couple. Sandra is a statuesque blonde with a purposeful stride. She has been an architect for a long time and, like many people lucky enough to be focused early in life, she is now rich thanks to regular clientele and some astute property investment.

Brian made his money specializing in orthodontics, and has found a niche amid zinc fillings, metal wire and plastic plates. His patrons are the rich matrons of Double Bay who sit in his surgery clasping the hands of their bucktoothed offspring, and find Brian's brown suits strangely comforting.

Sandra and Brian have a routine to their lovemaking. It begins with a series of signals. The first comes from Sandra, who puts on her flannel nightdress after a regime of skin care. It reminds her of boarding school. It makes her feel naughty. She then reclines on the bed and switches off the bedside lamp. Brian, dressed in his cotton shorts, obediently follows her cue.

The second signal involves Sandra suddenly wrapping her leg over Brian's torso, inadvertently brushing the tip of his penis. In the ensuing silence Sandra mounts the compliant Brian and rides him until she reaches orgasm. Brian's climax, a high-pitched whimper, usually follows a second later. Afterward she likes to get up to brush her teeth.

Sandra is larger than Brian and likes to be in control; Brian likes to think he enjoys being dominated. This is their equilibrium.

Sandra has just submitted a proposal with the Sydney City Council to design a museum to house firefighting equipment dating from the beginning of the colony. She has spent months drawing up her design. The council is to announce its decision about the museum that evening.

Sandra and Brian are dressed for the opera: Brian has donned a light summer suit in an unfortunate shade of beige and Sandra is in pink organza. Sandra sits by the phone, waiting. The heat makes her glisten. A fan spinning in the corner blows her hair away from her face. Her portfolio lies open on the desk. The drawing of the museum is a collision of swirling red arches and stark vertical chimneys thrusting up into a charcoal sky. It looks like fire, as if the building itself is struggling with the elements.

The phone rings. She jumps and grabs the receiver. Brian heads for the drinks cabinet—either way he is prepared to fix his wife a scotch. He watches her face as he pours the drink. Impenetrable, masklike, with only a light film of sweat betraying her. She answers the clerk on the other end of the line with short, polite affirmatives. It is this cool control of hers that Brian finds impossibly erotic. He watches the ice cubes tumble into the whisky then bob to the surface.

He hands her the scotch. She puts down the receiver slowly then swallows the drink in one gulp. She throws the glass against the white stippled wall. It just misses Brian's head.

"I've got it!" She dances around the fan, her pink organza fly-

ing. "I've got it!" Tentatively he reminds her that they are running late for the opera.

They get there just as the lights are dimming. It is a pro-
duction of Humperdinck's *Hansel and Gretel*. The director has
created a Gothic nightmare of epic proportions. From where
Sandra sits she can see the tenor sitting on a giant chair, his
feet swinging a good ten inches above the floor, his golden
curls and painted pink lips a pederast's dream. The witch trills
madly as she binds his feet and arms to the wooden limbs. As
the final knot is pulled tight Sandra feels a strange heat flooding her lower limbs. She looks at Brian, who is leaning forward,
face flushed, his tongue playing with the gap between his front
teeth. She looks back at the stage. The opera singer's legs lie
parted, tied to the chair with bright pink ribbon. Perhaps it is
the feeling of success that makes Sandra unusually aroused.
Perhaps it is the humidity that hangs like a collective mist over
the audience. Sandra suddenly finds the image of the singer
tied to the chair more than a little sexy.

In the dark, Brian's hand takes hers and places it firmly on
his growing erection. The witch throws back her head and
begins to sing, her bright red mouth stretched wide. Brian
throbs to a climax under Sandra's moving fingers.

The next night he brings home a length of pink ribbon.

Lying there afterward, her ankles and wrists stinging, her
body still warm from an orgasm whose voluminosity had surprised even herself, Sandra realizes they have stepped over a
boundary displacing their equilibrium. She glances over at
Brian, who lies with his back to her, his skin glistening.

The demands of Sandra's commission begin to dictate their
lives. She is in a frenzy, bent over cardboard models in which

the doorways yawn red, the turrets shoot up like flames and the external fire escape spirals down like drifting smoke. The more she scrawls her designs across the heavy draft paper, the more she feels her cells, her muscles, her juices thicken in expectation. The movement of her heavy pencil as it sweeps across the graph of her building suddenly holds the promise of a penis. A compass swing imagines tracings across a nipple. She wants her every orifice filled. She wants to lose control. To lose responsibility.

Every night, after hours of exhausting drafting and debate, she succumbs to Brian's little knots. His manipulation of her limbs makes her scream—stretching her, opening her—while the night breeze drifts in through the balcony doors, carrying faint shouts and the wailing of fire engines.

Sandra visits Brian during his lunch hour. Between the X rays, plaster casts of jaws and root-canal work she arrives, breathless. Brian, recognizing the click of her stilettos on the concrete steps of the fire escape, dismisses his assistant. Still wearing his white surgical gown, he leads Sandra by the hand to the dentist's chair. He ties her hands and ankles to the steel frame and gently places a gag in her mouth. He picks up a scalpel and cuts away at the crotch of her nylon tights. Kneeling, he hoists up the chair until her crotch is almost at eye level, then carefully splits her white underwear. With trembling fingers he folds the fabric back to reveal her Gold, as he calls her thick bush of blond pubic hair and cunt. To the sound of Stravinsky, he spreads her nether lips open and very slowly begins to snip away at the fringes of pubic hair around her vagina with tiny scissors, until the pink labia shine under the heat of the dentist's lamp. Brian pauses. Sandra is transformed. She trembles silently under his fingers. Her huge eyes roll above the gag. The only visible flesh is her vulva. Brian's hand brushes the tip of her clitoris. It flushes a deep red. Sandra revels in her helplessness. Brian, unaccustomed to this mute, malleable Sandra, fixes a small brush to the end of the drill. He bends down and, with one hand parting her labia, he caresses the tip of her clit with the spinning brush until she begs for mercy and comes, writhing, still tied and gagged to the chair.

The semen dries on the inside of Brian's thigh. Sandra takes a new pair of tights from her handbag and rolls them over her full, firm legs. She uses the reflective surface of the overhead lamp to apply her lipstick and adjust her hair. Completely clothed in a conservative grey suit with padded shoulders, her permed blond hair immaculate except for the curls that have stuck to her sweaty brow, she tucks her portfolio under her arm and heads out for an appointment with the Sydney City Council.

Brian watches her from the window and begins to grow hard again, thinking how no one would guess that this woman belonged to him, this dynamic controlled woman, who was, a minute ago, completely in his power.

Time is running out. Most nights Sandra comes in after eleven. She slips her clothes off and collapses exhausted on top of the blankets, still dressed in her underwear. Brian lies there, his eyes open, feeling her breath rise beside him. He wants to touch her but now all that is forbidden. Shut out, a part of him starts to hate her.

The closer the completion date of the building, the more distracted and obsessed Sandra becomes. Conversation evaporates. She can talk only of work, poured concrete and foundations. Brian thinks he is disappearing, fading into insignificance.

Soon their only real contact is during her lunchtime visits, when she is slave and he is master.

Her urgency consumes her. Her orgasms feed her work. Her work inflames her further. To save time, she has stopped wearing underpants and taken to wearing a garter belt. She has also shaved off her pubic hair. Everything is closer to the skin. As she walks through the council chambers in her high heels and long skirt she can feel the movement of her legs rub the spheres of her sex together. In a boardroom meeting, caught in a ring of men, she relishes her secret nakedness. Everything is designed to maximize the moment. The frenetic pace she lives her life has taken on a rhythm. This is her new equilibrium.

A man is perched on some scaffolding, just below a neon sign reading BERYL'S COOKIES ARE THE BEST. He sees a woman, beautiful at forty. She walks into a dentist's office in the building opposite. The man immediately senses something in her poise—her very gait—that suggests sex. As he draws closer, he fancies for a moment that he can smell through the glass, through the steel, sensing the rich pungent scent of her sex. Silently, out of view of his colleagues, he swiftly lets down the pulley so that his section of scaffolding is directly opposite the dentist's window. Hidden by a section of flimsy hardwood, he watches at his leisure the beautiful woman opposite whom he thinks is in love with a dentist. He watches as she walks into the center of the room and then lifts the edge of her skirt. The dentist walks up to her and pushes his hand roughly between her legs. It is as if the man can feel the damp imprint of her sex on his own wrist as the dentist pushes the woman toward the chair.

She falls slowly into it, her hair bouncing slightly on her

forehead as if in slow motion. The dentist opens the woman's legs with his rubber-gloved hands and ties her ankles to the chair. She puts up no struggle, but stares down at him with wide eyes. The man watching fancies he can see her bosom rising and falling in fear, in excitement, in submission. He moves closer to the hardwood panel and presses his erection against it. She has large breasts hidden under a tight white cotton blouse. It is this exterior of demure righteousness that pleases the watching man. He imagines that under the white cotton she would have long brown nipples that would harden against his teeth.

The dentist lifts her arms and ties her wrists to the head of the chair. The man watching would unbutton that blouse and release those full breasts. That's what he'd do. He would weigh them thoughtfully in each hand, then slowly run his thumb over those hardening nipples until they became erect. Then he would squeeze them firmly together and begin to suck at one and then the other until he could hear the woman moan. That's what he'd do if he was there. But the dentist seems only interested in touching the other. The best part. The bit he'd leave until last. The man watching reaches down and touches himself with his calloused hand, imagining the lips and tongue of the woman pulling down over the shaft of his penis, then over the knob with small circular motions, taking him deep into her throat. He always likes leaving the best part until the end.

Now the dentist has his face buried between the woman's legs. The man watching looks at the woman's face. Her cheeks are flushed and her eyes are rolling back in pleasure. She moves her arms backward and forward, chafing against the rope binding her to the chair. The man watching closes his eyes and comes against the grain of the wood. Every day after that he eats his lunch suspended in the little steel cage that hangs down the side of the building opposite the dentist's office.

It's now mid-December and the pressure on Sandra is immense. She feels as if her whole life is focused onto a thin point, and that thin point is the commission. Everyone else recedes, defined only by their function in relation to the execution of the building.

The more obsessed she becomes, the more Brian's anger ferments inside him. He hates the cardboard model of the museum, with its red turrets and display windows large enough to house several fire engines. He hates the way his wife burns with beauty as she manages four phone calls, two builders awaiting orders and a landscape gardener. He hates the way she has begun to look through people until they say words like *façade treatment, tilt slab* and *clerestory lighting.* He tries folding up his anger and slipping it between his gum and lip, but like an abscess it festers. He decides that he will confront her. He will force her to take a day off. But when he rings her office the line's engaged, when he tries the mobile the call is diverted, the fax is always busy.

He finds himself waiting for lunchtime. He finds that tying her down excites him more than fucking her. The equilibrium tilts back with the chair.

It is the end of summer. The reflective glass is now fitted to the steel frames, and the man's work is almost done. He sees a small blue BMW drive up a ramp and disappear into a parking lot in the street below. He smiles to himself and starts counting.

Twenty. He knows it takes twenty counts for her to be in the opposite building and seated in the dentist's chair.

Nineteen. "Just off for a smoke!" His mates smile knowingly. He climbs into the small steel cage and begins lowering the pulley by hand.

Fifteen. He can see her walking swiftly across the road, her blond hair white in the sunlight. He is excited by the knowledge that he alone knows where she is going and why. The pulley stops with a jolt. It sways slightly, then rests against the steel brackets. He squats close to the iron-mesh floor and stares into the office. The room is empty, the lamp is illuminating the vacant dentist's chair. The green of the leather shines, desolate and medicinal. He hates the dentist.

Five. She is at the door taking off her coat. She is hanging it carefully over the hook on the back of the door. The dentist enters. He walks up to the woman and pushes her over the dentist's chair. She falls, breasts forward, across the seat. He pushes his knee between her buttocks. As she is pinned to the seat, he grabs both her wrists and uses a towel to tie them crudely together.

Three. The dentist lifts up one thigh and pushes it over the arm of the chair. He ties the ankle to the outside frame. He then pushes her right thigh over the other arm and ties that ankle. Sandra is spread-eagled over the seat, her buttocks arched high in the air. Her face is pushed down into the seat. Brian rolls up her dress.

Two. She is wearing nothing but stockings.

One. He thinks she looks most beautiful like that. In surrender. He can see her elegant hands pressed up against each other almost in prayer. Her cheek is pushed down against the green leather. The man squatting in the steel cage thinks other women would lose their dignity tied up like that. But not her. He loves her for that. The way she stays dangerous even when tied up.

Brian steps back from his handiwork. His heart is pounding uncomfortably close to his throat. His wife's ass lies spread before him, the faintest wisp of blond hair framing anus and cunt. Beautiful. He can hear Sandra breathing. Her eyes are shut. He kneels and places his finger a millimeter above his wife's clitoris. He watches her grow erect. He wants her to say the word, he wants to hear her beg. He spreads her lips even farther apart and blows hard along the ridge of her clit. Sandra squirms. He can see the moisture collecting in the dark shadows. But she says nothing. Her silence makes him want to smack her hard across the ass. But he thinks this will give her pleasure, push her over the edge. He would like to take his cock out and press it against the rim of her asshole, gently teasing. Then plunge into her, feeling her arch in sudden pain. He does not. Like a mystic, he slowly runs his spread palms over the circumference of her, in the air above her skin. She is groaning now. He steps away and walks around to the other side of the chair. She looks up at him. Her eyes are blank animal. He wants her to say how much she wants him, needs him, to lose control. He pushes his fingers into her mouth and probes the inside of her gums, soft, wet. She sucks at his fingers, wanting.

"You want me, don't you? You need me, don't you?" She says nothing. He pulls his fingers out of her mouth. He kicks the base of the chair. It spins around. Her body rotates with it like a crazy merry-go-round. He watches her, her torso swinging from shadow to light from light to shadow like day to night. She doesn't cry out, but accepts this chaotic world as if it were her penance. The chair stops spinning. Brian buries his face into her cunt. He sucks and licks her until she is close to bursting.

Suddenly he stands. He takes off his white smock and hangs it over her leather coat and leaves the room. The door slams behind him.

The man in the steel cage watches the dentist leave the room. The woman is still tied over the chair. He looks down at the street. The dentist, his bald head a pink map, walks across the street then into the car park. The man's heart begins to hammer. He looks back at the room. The vulnerability of the woman tightens his loins, his cock lies hard in the leg of his shorts. Slowly he begins to slide the steel cage down to the ground.

Sandra lies motionless. She can feel the heat of the lamp on her back. She is listening hard for her husband's footsteps. She hopes he's in the adjoining room, although she has already heard him disappear down the corridor and into the lift. The presence of him in the other room is an irrational illusion, but she holds on to it to stop herself from screaming. She struggles with the ropes but he has tied her firmly. It is impossible to escape. She lies there open to the world. It is then that she hears the click of the door.

"Brian?" With her face against the seat, Sandra cannot see him. The footsteps are heavy. He comes up behind her. His hands are on her. They run down the sides of her buttocks to her pussy. He opens her lips, his thumb on her clit. Strange hands, heavier than Brian's, the skin rough like a cat's tongue. He rubs her gently. The strangeness of this man excites her. His smell is different, he smells dark, as if he has more body hair. Like soil, with a faint tinge of machine oil underneath. She feels the dull weight of his cock against her thigh. He enters her slowly. He is bigger than Brian and she stretches with his thickness. She gasps as he starts to increase his rhythm. Pushing his large hands under her skirt, he releases her breasts, pulling at the nipples. He reaches up and unties the knots around her wrists. He pulls her upright and down onto his lap, cupping her breasts as she rides him, and biting the back of her neck. She feels the mouth she hasn't yet seen— full and strong, the bottom lip jutting over the top. She twists to see him but he firmly keeps her facing away.

The dentist chair tilts back like a bed. He pushes her down, so that her face is near his knees. He moves her legs so that they run up along his hips to his shoulders. She is lying flat against his body. His cock is still inside her, pushing against the back of her sex. They move slowly. From his reclining position he can see where he is entering her. He parts her buttocks, gently easing two fingers into her ass. She moans and claws at his legs as she swells towards orgasm. She reaches back and clutches at his clothes, her fingers tracing an embroidered insignia. McGillis. Squeezing her breasts, he thrusts into her. She cannot hold back any longer and her orgasm rips through her. She cries out as she feels him contracting with her.

The movement of her head triggers the X-ray machine. It extends its lens automatically before taking another image.

The next day Sandra is driving her blue BMW down a highway in the western suburbs. It is a humid day, the traffic is heavy. The working drawings are on the seat beside her. As she waits at a red light she glances across at them. They look impressive, blue and pink ink trace the three-dimensional proportions of the museum, a maze of column grid and footing details. She drives into the car park of the warehouse. A sign stretches over the gateway: McGillis building corporation, Est. 1972. She has arrived.

Brian is leaning over Elsa, an attractive patient in her early thirties. As Brian taps her tooth with a dental pick, Elsa winces in pain. His assistant enters the room and touches him on the shoulder. She has Elsa's dental X rays as he requested, but there is something else. He excuses himself, leaving Elsa wide-eyed, her mouth braced open. He follows his assistant into the next room. Silently she pins the X ray against the light. Two pelvic bones, one male, one female, are visible. The bases of both spines and two pubic bones are pushed together, bumping like white bats in the dark.

"Fucking," he mutters under his breath.

"Sorry?" the assistant asks, not trusting her ears.

"Fucking. It's an X ray of fucking," Brian pronounces clearly, while instinctively twisting the wedding ring on his finger.

Sandra spreads out the drawings on the executive's desk. He is the chief foreman of the construction company. Over a hundred men work under him. As she bends over, he notices her cleavage and the soft texture of her hair.

"I'd better call Robert, he's handling this job." He speaks into an intercom. She glances around the office. A girlie calendar on one wall, featuring the famous porn star Candy Perkins, advertises concrete; a photo of the wife and baby granddaughter sit on the desk. Through the glass partition, Sandra can see the workers moving large sheets of wood across the warehouse floor.

"Robert's the best in the business, you'll be okay with him."

She recognizes his aroma before she sees him, a lingering concoction of sweat, hair and a residue of aftershave. The same smell. Her heart races, she feels herself responding in scent.

She looks up. His face betrays nothing as he extends a hand. He squeezes her hand slightly as they shake. He is younger than she thought. His eyes are an intense blue. The hair on his chest curls over the white T-shirt under his blue overalls. He catches her looking at his body.

As she takes him through the drawings he listens quietly. His hands, heavy workman's hands, slowly caress the lines of the museum, working their way through the collision of masculine and feminine, the vertical and the arched.

Outside the office he offers to drive her to the site.

"Only if I'm in control," she says and smiles slowly.

MAN OF SIGHS

I'd never been one for revenge. The moralist in me always considered it too calculating and too undignified. Until I fell in love with Humphrey. Then I transformed into Medea, Jezebel and the Wicked Witch of the West overnight.

I had been celibate for six months—a reaction to a broken love affair. One of those sordid triangles full of illusion and desire, made more attractive by my unavailability. Naturally, I ceased to be so alluring when the girlfriend got pregnant. Suddenly cut free, I felt abandoned and bruised. I went into retreat, developing casual friendships with two men I'd meet for coffee. I flirted with the idea of sleeping with them, but decided I couldn't trust the emotional consequences of any sexual involvement. I should have known then.

One of the men was a journalist—a laconic, self-effacing chap with an acidic wit. Coffee with him was like a visit to the analyst, involving much self-deprecation and a mutual despairing of Sydney society. His misanthropic sensibility was not a great sexual turn-on.

The other man was Humphrey. Coffee with Humphrey usually took place in complete silence. Defiantly glamorous and

single, I'd wait for him at some bar in Taylor Square, surrounded by waiters—beautiful and homosexual—fluttering
above me like exotic butterflies engrossed in their dramatic
worlds of fecund attractions.

Humphrey would appear, dressed in some self-made con-
traption like sandals made of tire rubber tied with string, his
face still smeared with paint, his hair covered in sawdust, his
large rough hands stained with oil. Standing silently by the
bar, he would watch me waiting for him. Then his scent would
always give him away. Pungent and slightly oily, it would drift
across and I'd swing around and see him in all his maleness,
grinning his sardonic smile, his ageing, pock-marked skin still
handsome. Humphrey was an original.

Humphrey's reputation as a notorious womanizer made me
curious. I didn't consciously find him attractive, but I found the
idea of so many women falling under the spell of this odd and
in some ways shy man fascinating. In the same way I found certain insects fascinating. There was even a rumor that the sound
of the orgasms of all the women he'd ever made come followed
him around like a faint echo, like the ocean trapped in a
seashell. Besides, he found me attractive. I liked that; it
restored my battered confidence.

Humphrey was an artist. Primarily a sculptor. You can divide
sculptors into two categories, ones that subtract to arrive at the
form and ones that build to create form. Humphrey was a sub-
tractor, as if he instinctively knew the shape that was trapped
beneath the stone, the lump of clay, hidden under knots of
wood. I'd been to his studio once and watched him free one of
his figures. Thin and nubile, she emerged from the pink marble like a woman shaking out her hair in sunlight. I watched
him working on the piece, polishing the marble as if it were

skin, drawing out the shape as if he were pulling at his own flesh. His large, heavy hands spoke of work, of instinct, bypassing intellect altogether. I guess this was one of the things I was drawn to, this communication through the flesh.

Humphrey was not a storyteller. When he did speak, it was in short, cryptic sentences or, on occasion, long monologues of lateral witty observations. When he was younger he used to stutter, so badly that until the age of thirty he was practically incomprehensible. Perversely, I found that irresistible.

It was the end of summer, a hot night when all of Darlinghurst goes in search of a party. The humidity gets under the skin and creates a sexual friction, and before you know it the streets are crawling with people in search of some kind of contact—the brush of fingertips, a kiss, anything. I was in huntress mode, adorned to swallow some man up. Dressed in a blue skintight number, stretched tightly across my breasts and pulled down to expose my shoulders, I felt hot. Let's face it, I *was* hot, my vows of celibacy evaporating every time my garter belt rubbed against my thighs.

The party was held in a converted garage, tucked away behind high offices and a desolate row of terraces abandoned by the city planners. The basement had been transformed into a dance floor complete with colored lights, a strobe and a sound system that pounded off the walls. There must have been about three hundred people crowded into this tiny, hot building. I pushed my way through the usual collection of faces—students, journalists, fashion models, unemployed actors, junkies and would-be film directors—down toward the dance floor.

The walls sweated as people gyrated their bodies like fish in a tank. To one side of me was a lesbian couple. One of the women, resplendent in chain mail, bright red cropped hair and Viking helmet, slithered down the glistening body of her partner. Behind me a young man in sixties bell-bottoms cradled his fourteen-year-old girlfriend. Next to them a man in his fifties, dripping with love beads and feathers, undulated in his own time warp. The whole place was bouncing with a kind of child-like abandonment.

I could feel men watching me. The hunger in their faces made me wet. Ignoring them, I continued to dance on my own. The music coursed through my blood and up through my womb. It was like dancing in thick honey.

There was that scent again. Faint but totally distinctive, it floated past my face. I opened my eyes to find Humphrey dancing in front of me. Normally clumsy, he had real grace. He moved as if he was making love; every movement instinctive and sure. He wove himself around me for hours, caressing the air between us.

Outside, dawn had turned the sky a pale gray. Humphrey, not daring to presume anything, offered to walk me home. As we all know, momentous events start in the most arbitrary way; destiny doesn't really offer us a choice. It's a trick God plays. In this instance it started with my bursting bladder. Hobbling along in my high heels, full of beer, I realized I'd have to stop off at Humphrey's place.

His flat was in an old Victorian block, bleak in red brick. I had always resisted visiting him there, feeling that the proximity might have an inevitability to it. A sexual fatality.

The room was dark, with a few broken pieces of furniture. There was a model of a heart resting on a picture frame, one of those three-dimensional plastic replicas of the organ. I remember I brought it down and began to open it up. He told me it was a present from his last lover, who had fled to England a week before. He seemed to find the plastic organ an apt metaphor for their relationship. I didn't bother probing, but now I wish that I had. In the center of the room was a beautiful wooden model of a sailing yacht. It stood about four foot in height, with miniature rigging and brass fittings bolted to the deck. It seemed to be the only cherished object in the room. Humphrey watched me as I gravitated toward it. As I bent over the polished stern I could feel him wanting me from the other side of the room. I liked that, teasing the moment out before we touched for the first time.

He came up silently behind me. I stood pinned, feeling like a deer caught in the glare of headlights. He lifted my long hair and bit into the back of my neck. I could feel his teeth as he breathed in the smell of my hair, my body. We stood there for aeons, caught in that dangerous impasse between friendship and lust. I could feel his cock, hard in the small of my back. My head rolled against his shoulder, resting in the hollow of his neck. In the silence, I swear I heard a faint gasp, a woman's breath caught in pleasure. Man of sighs, I thought, he is a man of sighs.

There are two kinds of men: those who are cunt-shy and those who are not. Those who are not are the connoisseurs who know where a woman likes to be worshipped. And Humphrey was the ultimate connoisseur, a sex artist, one of those rare men who was able to focus completely when making love to a woman. He was totally intuitive about what I wanted when weaving his naked body around mine. It was as if he was able to second-guess my fantasies.

He squatted over me, his cock moving slowly in me,
between my closed legs. He threw back his head and I had the
definite impression that he was in direct communion with the
great god Pan. There was a complete abandonment of intellect
in his lovemaking, as if he was tapping into a higher frenetic
power. I was drunk with his tongue, his cock, his lips, the hair
on the back of his neck, his hands and the danger of it all.
What could I do? I fell heavily headfirst like all the women
before me. Love is like vertigo. I know, I suffered from it—as a
child I couldn't even cross bridges. Falling in love with a friend
is disastrous, it's like stepping into a shower that you know will
scald you.

There was no way I could plead ignorance, after all I'd been
warned about his previous conquests, his tendency to evaporate at the mention of commitment. And hadn't it been me he'd
confided in over all those coffees?

We were lovers for three months. In those days I was working
for the Ministry of Planning and Environment as a consultant
for salinity. After days of touring around the barren districts of
New South Wales, photographing the white crusty rims of
saltbeds, visiting the local church halls and standing in front of
suspicious beery men twenty years my senior to lecture them
about the dangers of over-farming, chemical insecticides and
blue algae, I'd find myself stumbling down Oxford Street, still
dressed in my pin-striped suit, heading toward his apartment.

Humphrey would open the door without questioning my
sudden arrival, take my briefcase from me, sit me down in front
of the television and present me with a plate of spaghetti or
paella, the only two dishes he knew how to cook. I'd sit there
eating, losing myself in some disaster in Eastern Europe or

graphic car crash in Newcastle, but still acutely conscious of him moving around behind me. The very space between us was erotic. Once, after finishing my meal, I put my hand to the back of my hair and found he was pressing his erect penis into my tresses. Humphrey loved my hair; he called it the hair of Eve, loving the scent, the weight of it.

I don't think he thought in language at all, but in images that were juxtaposed like some mad surrealist painting. He exuded an electricity that disrupted the linear in nature: plates would crash to the ground, thunderstorms would suddenly break out when he was around.

He would take me on the bare wooden floorboards, lifting my skirt to part my lips and pay homage to my vulva, finding every possible caress with his tongue, teeth and lips, taking me to the brink for hours before finally entering me with his blunt, hard cock. Afterward we would lie there twisted, exhausted, sated, my head against his foot, my back upside down against the corner of the room, his knee in my mouth, his cock in my elbow. When the silence became uncomfortable he would pluck out my pubic hair from between his teeth and tell me about his sexual escapades.

Early one morning when the streets were still desolate, with only the party-goers gliding past the pimps, the homeless and the desperate, while a flock of cockatoos shrieked above like a thousand rancorous drag queens flapping their way over Kings Cross, Humphrey was stopped by a traveler when returning home from a lover. The man asked for the way to Central Station. Humphrey obliged and began to trace a map in the dust of the pavement. Suddenly he noticed the man staring strangely at his face. Humphrey, who was used to being stared at, continued on regardless. Eventually, the man excused himself and rushed away. Humphrey, bemused, walked on and in that hazy, muddled morning state soon forgot the man's fear.

Back at home he started dressing and was about to leave when he checked to see if he needed to shave. Shocked, he noticed a huge smear of dried blood across his mouth and cheek. For a moment he tried to remember whether he had cut himself, until he realized that it was the menstrual blood of the woman he had just left. The man's staring face suddenly made sense.

I loved that story, and imagined all sorts of romantic notions of Humphrey brazenly wearing that stain as a mark of woman. The imprint of woman on a man who loved women.

At work, in the middle of a slide show illustrating the merits of irrigation, the scent of Humphrey would miraculously drift across the room, carried along by the smell of mown grass blowing in from an open window. I would find myself faltering in front of a group of cynical wheat farmers as the lines of irrigation on the slide dissolved into the line of black hairs running up from erect cock to navel. I felt as if I was in the grip of some crazed sexual alchemist. The more I had him, the more I wanted him. My visits to his apartment became a nightly occurrence. Sometimes he would already be asleep, half-drunk, murmuring no, no, as I took him into my mouth, slowly winning him over with my tongue. At other times it would be me falling onto his disheveled bed with the red dust of the soil still in my hair. He would work over my body in the same way he drew shape out of a stone.

My fascination with his past moved from the objective to the subjective. I could no longer listen to stories of sexual duplicity and deceit without identifying with the female victim. For the first time in my life I felt as if I understood the phrase "you have undone me." Humphrey had achieved it very simply, without words, without psychology. I had made the fatal mistake of believing in his touch, as if the intelligence of his hands, our orgasms, the way he penetrated me, had affected him as much as it had affected me. Perhaps this is the catch cry of the egoist: I love, therefore I must be loved. Perhaps it is the Achilles heel of my gender.

I became possessive. As we all know, the way to retain a wolf's interest is to feign complete indifference, to keep for oneself a kernel of dignity, of independence. I've always had a policy of placing myself and my autonomy first. That way I had survived all the sudden departures, deaths, deceits and emotional ambiguities. Until Humphrey.

Like all conquest junkies, Humphrey had begun to detect the stale smell of victory. Soon he stopped returning my calls. Sometimes I'd arrive at his apartment sweating in panic, having imagined all sorts of scenarios as I walked from my place to his. I'd bang on the door, knowing that his light was on, but he'd just sit in silence, refusing to answer my knocking. Furious, I would ring for hours from a nearby telephone booth, as the street-cleaning van crawled along the empty streets. He was cutting me out of his life, neatly, like a piece of marble falling away from a fault line. Humphrey's sense of time and place was finite. Women belonged to certain periods of history that, once experienced and consumed, were then obsolete.

At first I refused to believe that our intimacies meant nothing to him. My ego wouldn't allow it; my instinct couldn't rationalize it. Then a terrible anger set in. I felt as if I had been poisoned. I wanted to put him through as much pain as I was going through. I wanted revenge.

*   *   *

I first met Elsa at a cocktail bar situated above a gay pub on the corner of Taylor Square, one of those Sydney locations that ran the whole gamut of sexuality in the course of a Friday night. The parties started at five with happy hour, when the half-price drinks attracted the heterosexual office workers in their short-sleeved shirts and shoulder pads, to be replaced by the local gay community two hours later. Many of the lesbians were only distinguishable by the nipples poking up beneath pristine white T-shirts, their cropped hair reflecting the style of their male counterparts. It was the beginning of the era of lipstick dykes, when the audacious anti-beauty stance of the older separatists was slowly being replaced by a whole gener-ation of highly fashionable gay women celebrating the blatant sexuality of their scarlet-painted mouths.

I was marooned there, waiting for Humphrey to turn up. Happy hour came and went, and gradually the tables were replaced by boys and their men, girls and their women. I found myself staring into my vodka, trying to adopt an exterior of nonchalance, while my heterosexuality flashed like neon over my head: straight, straight, straight.

It was then that Elsa walked in. She had the kind of grace that turned heads, as if you had caught the flight of some trop-ical bird in your peripheral vision. She was tall, with black hair that fell to her shoulders, high cheekbones, heavy eyebrows and green eyes a shade I'd never seen before. It was as if she had no iris. Her large breasts swung free under a loose T-shirt of thin white silk, below which a pair of leather jodhpurs cut angularly across her hips. She made her way past the tables and pinched the bottom of the transvestite waitress before throwing herself down in the chair next to me.

"Don't get paranoid," she said, "I know you're straight."

I felt Elsa looking at me, her eyes surreptitiously sliding down my body, leaning forward, finding reasons to touch my thigh or brush her naked arm against mine, her musk settling over me like a hypnotic mist. I knew she wanted me. More than that, Elsa was the type of woman who was used to getting what she wanted. To be desired by those who are themselves highly desirable is in itself an aphrodisiac. I found myself wondering how easy it would be to reach across and slip a hand under the thin silk, to feel the weight of her breast cupped in my hand, to bite suddenly into that luscious flesh.

By the time Humphrey arrived we were drunk, and firm allies. Humphrey noticed her immediately, assessing her youth, her body, her beauty in one glance. Faking indifference, he could hardly look her in the eye, but I knew that glimmer, that glint as he glanced surreptitiously across at her. I watched as he licked his lips, measuring his silences carefully, projecting that fatal broodiness. He performed for Elsa, while Elsa performed for me. It was perfect.

Obsession is an interesting thing: to be the object of obsession is empowering; to be obsessive is totally disempowering. Later that night, Elsa phoned me and made a date for coffee. After she rang, Humphrey phoned me asking for her number. A plan began to form in my mind. Elsa was like that, one of those rare moments of beautiful synchronicity that left me contemplating my atheism.

One day, Elsa invited me over to her apartment, an elegant unit overlooking Woolloomooloo Bay. There were three erotic Chinese prints on the wall. The first was of an older, Buddha-like man sitting behind a beautiful young girl, plump, with childlike features. He had her legs spread far apart, as if offering her up to the world. Her reddened sex was detailed in tiny brush strokes, the lips curling like a budding peony. Both had innocent smiles of intense pleasure.

The second was of the same couple, only in this print the man had curved his body over her; he was still smiling, with two spots of red in his cheeks. She had taken his penis into her mouth, while he was delicately inserting his tongue into her. He looked as if he was consuming a rare delicacy. As I stared, I was convinced that I could detect a trembling in her plump, parted thighs as if she was on the brink of orgasm.

"I'm a collector of erotica," Elsa smiled. "Straight or gay, doesn't affect the value of the prints. I've made quite a bit of money this way, buying up and selling again. I sell to anyone: galleries, private collectors, concert halls—."

She handed me a drink, settling down on the couch. "So tell me, how long has Humphrey been your lover?"

I smiled slowly. If Elsa wasn't going to have me, she was determined to have me vicariously. She wanted to know how we made love, how often and in what positions. It was as if she was trying to develop a palette of what I found sexually stimulating. So I told her about the time we went to the country.

We'd been swimming down at the ocean that day with a group of friends. I remember being sandwiched against Humphrey in the car on the trip back. The heat of the sun was beating in through the car window, the warmth of my burnt skin prickling under my T-shirt. The sensation of his thigh against mine and the secrecy of our love affair excited me greatly, but he deliberately withheld himself as he sat beside me in silence. Suddenly, he told the driver to stop and let us out right there, in the middle of the bush. The car screeched to a halt. Our friends were used to Humphrey's eccentricity.

Smiling but without comment they drove off, leaving us standing by the side of the road. Anticipation made my heart into a drum.

"Walk," Humphrey's tone was different, commanding. I had never heard him sound so aggressive. It excited me, yet I was almost afraid. I started to walk in front of him through the bushes. I could feel his eyes touching me, slipping their way into my sex. Everywhere around me seemed to reflect my hunger, my wetness for him. The wattle's faint but sticky scent, the hovering bees probing the blooms, the constant droning of the insects—all seemed to stream back into my body, ripening it. I stumbled and half turned.

"Don't look at me." His voice jerked me back to reality. We arrived at a small clearing. A large water tower shot up through the trees, the silver tank catching the light of the sun.

"Up against the tower," Humphrey ordered. I obeyed him and leaned against the corrugated surface.

He came up behind me, and roughly parted my thighs with his knee, forcing me to spread my legs. He pulled down my jeans, and sank to the grass. Parting me I could feel the soft wetness of his tongue as he probed me gently, his nails sinking into my cheeks. The contrast between the gentleness of his tongue and the sharpness of his nails was intense. He stood and slipped his cock between my legs, rubbing the shaft across my clit then drawing it up against my asshole. He reached around and slipped a finger into my cunt, then touched my clit. Suddenly he thrust into me. I thought he would split me. My face was pushed up against the hot tin, the size of him filling me, as he plunged over and over. We came together, loudly, as above us a kookaburra burst into hysterical laughter.

"A little pain mixed in with the pleasure is always a good thing." Elsa grinned, dipping her finger into her vodka and sucking it reflectively.

Humphrey had started to follow Elsa through the streets in his old white van. Her phone would ring in the middle of the night; he'd listen to her voice, just for a second, before hanging up. She knew it was him from the splattering inhalation of breath, and she was sure he was masturbating. She told me, with a certain mixture of pity and repulsion, that he had been seen standing for hours in the bookstore she worked in, just looking through the magazines.

Elsa watched me carefully for a reaction. I knew she was searching for a sign that I was still deeply involved. I kept my face and voice completely neutral, although inwardly the very mention of Humphrey's name sent shock waves through my body, my heart pounding to the point of nausea. The more she rejected him, the more he wanted her. For a man who'd had every woman he'd ever desired, rejection was proving to be the greatest thrill of all.

By this time, although I knew I had lost him completely, I couldn't exorcise his scent. I would masturbate and be left with the smell of him on my fingers. I couldn't look at other men. I began to hate him, and my desire for revenge became overwhelming.

Elsa decided to commission Humphrey, and insisted that I act as a go-between. She had given him free range of material and medium but wanted the subject to be herself. Humphrey's face lit up in anticipation. He was almost salivating. It was a pathetic sight.

*   *   *

We meet outside his studio, a large Victorian warehouse.
Humphrey occupies the top floor, which he has converted into
an open white space. White silk hangs over the bay windows,
giving a radiance to the light that shines through them. He has
defined the studio as a sacred place.

Elsa presses the buzzer. Humphrey's voice sounds tentative
over the intercom—I have never heard him sound so uncer-
tain. I start to feel a little more powerful. As we go up in the
lift, Elsa hugs me and tells me to relax.

But Humphrey's face falls when he sees me standing behind
Elsa. He leads us into the main part of the studio. A canvas is
set up on an easel, and an old bed swathed in sheets stands in
the center of the room.

"I want something that represents physical decay. Death and
the maiden—know what I mean, Elsa?" He turns to her, avoiding my eyes completely. Elsa smiles slowly, like a sphinx.

"I know exactly what you mean." She picks up a piece of
white chalk and draws a large circle around the easel and his
palette.

"Stand in there."

"What?"

"I choose the conditions and I want you to stand in there."
Humphrey steps inside the circle.

"You're not allowed to step outside, understand?" He
nods slowly and picks up his paintbrush. Elsa leads me over
to the bed.

"Take your clothes off." I begin to move toward the bathroom, but she grabs my arm. Hard.

"Here. Take your clothes off here." She undoes the top button of my shirt and sits on the bed to watch. I begin to strip.
At first shyly, but, feeling the other two watching me, I begin

to take on the persona of a performer, unbuttoning my shirt
slowly, then the skirt and finally throwing off my tights. I stop
at my bra and underpants. Elsa stubs out her cigarette.

"Those too."

"No!"

A cool hand curls around my waist. "Do it."

Slowly I unhook my bra. As I turn I can see Humphrey sitting on a stool beside his easel. He stares at my body as if he
has never seen it before. Elsa stands behind me, turning my
body toward him for display. She touches the tips of my
breasts until they become erect. I can hear Humphrey's
breathing become heavier. I shut my eyes. I feel Elsa's hands
as they slip down the contours of my body toward my
underpants.

"Open your legs." Like a sleepwalker I obey her. Parting my
legs slightly, she pushes her arm roughly between my thighs
and pulls the underpants down. I am damp. Humphrey lurches
forward out of the circle, but Elsa swings around violently,
yelling, "Move—and it's over!"

She stands between me and the white chalk circle, teasing,
knowing the full control she has over her spectators. She
begins to peel off her clothes very, very slowly. I watch
Humphrey's face, pale and trembling, his mouth twitching
slightly as behind me I hear the thud of her jeans as they hit
the floor, her T-shirt thrown down carelessly, her white lace
bra flung over the bed and finally her underpants, which she
takes off and places so very daintily at the edge of the chalk
circle. She stands for a moment in her nakedness, lifting her
arms above her head and pivoting in the parody of a ballerina.
Her long, firm legs lead up to two ripe cheeks. Her ass is small
but firm, her waist tiny, her ribs ripples of light. The most fem-

inine thing about her are those full mother's breasts, no hint of
any sexual ambiguity there.

Humphrey looks as if he is about to spring but he remains
within the chalk circle. Elsa sticks her tongue out at him, bending it back provocatively. He moves to the edge of the circle,
his whole body stretching forward in an attempt to meet hers.

"One more step and you're a dead man!" Elsa screams at him.
He stops, his erection visible in his baggy trousers. "Want me?
Smell me? Want both of us? Suffer, boy . . ."

Humphrey reaches over and dips his brush into a pigment.
Lifting it out of the paint, it drips scarlet. He stands in front of
the easel poised, ready for the first mark to be scrawled across
the virgin canvas. Elsa moves across the polished wooden
floor, her feet making soft thuds as she runs toward me. She
lifts me up in her arms in one effortless movement. As she cradles me I can see the muscles strain in her upper arm. She car-
ries me over to the bed and places me on it. I lie on my side,
waiting, impassive under her fingers.

"Pose number one." She gets up on the bed. Kneeling
behind me, she pulls me up so that I face Humphrey. She
wraps her legs around my waist. I can feel the fur of her sex
against the small of my back, the tip of her clitoris a fleshy spot
that sticks to my skin. She parts me with her feet. Wide. So
wide I am forced to lie back onto her with my head resting
between her breasts. She runs her hands around my back and
under my breasts, cupping them between her thumb and fore-
finger. The pose I recognize from the Chinese etchings, pose
number one. Elsa is enacting her favorite image. We sit like
that for five minutes. An eternity lapses and I find myself wanting to be taken by both of them.

Humphrey sweeps in bold red arcs across the canvas; the

curve of the two backs arch over each other, the slash of my cunt between Elsa's two feet. By pulling her feet farther apart, she pulls my lips back. I can feel my clit swell and lift, wanting to be touched. Tempting Humphrey. He crouches over, pathetic, holding himself, his wide-open eyes eating everything up.

Delicately, she begins to touch me with her toes, pulling gently at me as I become wet between her feet. She has me pinned. I don't want Humphrey to see that I am close to coming, so I roll my head back, taking one of Elsa's nipples into my mouth, tasting salt and feeling her grow erect as I tease with my teeth.

Humphrey bends over the easel, maniacally splashing paint in great sprays. He eases his cock out of his fly; it stands erect, absurd against the cotton of his trousers. He holds it in his left hand, running his fingers along the whole shaft, pulling down over the tip. The paint brush in his right hand pushes huge globules of paint over the surface in rhythm with his left.

Elsa lifts her legs away from me and kneels on the floor. I move forward so that I am curled over her body. She turns me around so that my pudendum is facing Humphrey.

"Pose number two." She places me in the position of the young Chinese girl in the second picture; there is a precision to her actions as she orchestrates the making of the image. Her hands slide around the orbs of my ass. She pries me open, turning my secret parts into a visual feast. I sit over her face and can feel her breath on my thighs. One finger slides into my ass while two others enter my cunt, and she pulls me down to her mouth. Her tongue touches the tip of my clit, teasing, flicking. Humphrey groans, almost weeping with frustration. I can see his hands trembling, the sweat beading on his face.

Elsa lies spread below me. Tentatively I run my hands along her legs. Silk. Such young skin. Her jet-black pubic hair lies in wisps, almost Asian in its sparseness. I can see her lips through the hair. Gently, I pull back her outer lips and feel her moisten, her clit a cherry.

The room fills with our groaning. From between Elsa's legs I can see Humphrey kneeling at the edge of the chalk circle, his back arched, his trousers down to his knees, his cock hard and shiny rising up through his fist. He leans forward, getting as close as he can to our bodies without crossing the chalk boundary. I can feel his breath on my back. Elsa shoves two more fingers into my ass, taking my whole cunt into her mouth. She licks my lips then pulls back, sucking my clit.

Slowly I lower my face into her sex, tasting her clit with my tongue. Salty. Clean. I want to give her pleasure. I take her whole clit and play it across my tongue. I can feel her stiffen. More. I dig my nails into the cheeks of her ass and start sucking vigorously.

Humphrey is close to coming, his cock enormous. A huge red pole rolling between his hands. Kneeling at the edge of the circle, he suddenly lashes his paint brush through the air. The yellow paint splashes up between our bodies. Elsa smears the paint across my breasts, drawing her own breasts across my belly. The paint feels wet and sticky.

Humphrey watches in anger. Impotent, he flings another dash of paint across my back. Blue drips down between my buttocks and onto Elsa's forehead. She smears it down over my ass and down the outside of my thighs. The streak of blue across her forehead has transformed her into a frenzied warrior queen.

She massages the blue into the yellow, masking me. I can

feel the paint solidify as it dries slowly, pulling back my skin. She has given me a mask. She has given me a license to be different.

We roll over and over, landing in a pool of green paint. She's on top now, her cunt spread above me. She manipulates me so that I slip up and down in the pool of paint as she pulls at my cunt with her mouth. The paint oozes between everything, between my fingers, between my toes, between my legs.

Humphrey, now also naked and splattered with color, pulls at himself furiously. He rolls back his head in the way I know so well, in the throes of Pan. But I don't want him to come, I don't want him to come with us.

I push my fingers into Elsa and take her clit between my teeth. We both start to come, and I am barely able to keep her in my mouth when Humphrey suddenly spurts a jet of sperm over the chalk border and across the room. It spills across my skin in a thin, hot stream.

In the silence afterward we all start to laugh. Revenge—I was always lousy at it.

THE MAN WHO LOVED SOUND

Two men. One, large, on the brink of middle age, leans against an open window, smoking. Outside the afternoon traffic roars past, sending up clouds of dust into the sunlight that cuts into the dingy lounge room. He flicks ashes on the carpet.

The second man, thin, crouches by a record player, his long arms wrapped around his knees. He rocks himself backward and forward over the worn rug, trying to stop himself from crying.

The fat man leans across and squeezes the other's skinny shoulder.

The man in black denim stands slowly, swaying on his feet.

QUIN

My name's Quin, "the Wolf" to some. They call me that because of my hair. I haven't brushed it in years. That doesn't mean that it isn't clean. It is. I like to keep it clean for the ladies. They like to weave their fingers through it and pull hard, especially when they're coming. I keep it matted, like an animal's. A wild, untamed animal. That's why they call me the Wolf.

I don't say much. I don't need to. When I'm standing at the

back of some gig in the dark with the music washing over me I'm in paradise. And the women sense it, they come to me without me even having to move a muscle. Instinct, that's what they love, a man who knows his own pleasure.

MACK

I first saw Quin at a recording session. It was in the late seventies and I was twenty-six, young enough to still get excited when I heard those guitar riffs pounding at the studio window. I can't remember the band now, but I remember Quin. He was curled up on the floor, crouching against the wall. His eyes were closed and that demented hair was snaking all over the large nose, the oily skin, the bat ears. Jerking rhythmically to the music, he looked like a gypsy violinist in a wedding somewhere in Prussia last century. I remember leaning across and shouting in the singer's ear, "Get the fucking junkie out!" All the singer did was smile.

"Quin, what were the last four bass chords?"

Quin didn't even bother to open his eyes. "A, E, B and F sharp."

That's my man, best ears in the industry grafted onto the body of a spider.

QUIN

I don't like to say much in case I miss something. I like listening—to every nuance, every tonal gradation. I live through my ears. The first thing I can remember is the sound of a beer can being ripped open, my Irish father celebrating my birth with a toast. In the background I could detect the rat-tat-tat of Yiddish as my mother, Esther, organized my circumcision with my grandfather. Some people have really sharp eyesight, others can feel emotions with their fingers. Me, I hear everything. Sometimes I think I can hear the ants in the soil. Mack thinks it's a gift. I think it's a handicap: I hear too much.

Music is different: It's color. It's blue laced with silver. It's lightning in a storm. It's an orgasm through the veins. When I'm listening to music, I shut my eyes and pretend that my body is cat-gut stretched over a drum. In moments like this I am nothing but pure vibration. In moments like this I forget thought.

That's why I've dedicated my life to music, to the recording and preservation of acoustic beauty. I put that in my résumé when I applied for the job at Mack's studio. That's why he employed me, so he can point me out to visiting artists and say, "That's Quin. Mention digital audio technology around him and he'll cut your balls off, but if you're into acoustics he's the best in Australia."

Mack's a victim of history. He solidified years ago, but he respects me. I like that. It gives me somewhere to touch down.

MACK

Digital audio technology. Yeah, been around for a while and it ain't going away. Quin loathed it with a vengeance. He said it minimized sound, flattened it and spat it out onto a disk at the other end. He blamed the media giants and fabricated his own conspiracy theory. But what could I do? I'm a businessman. I had business to do and the clients wanted the latest. So I converted all the studios to DAT—all except Quin's. Maybe I have a soft spot for the past. Superstition has always been my weak-

ness; my old dad used to say, a little bit of the past will help
with the future. Dad used to sell clothes wringers under Central Station. Then they introduced washing machines and he
went bankrupt. Anyway, Quin had become a mascot for the
studio, and mascots have their uses.

QUIN

My homemade record player has twelve valves that all glow in
the dark. Little red throbbing beacons. It takes half an hour to
warm them up before I can put the needle down on the spinning black disc. I only listen to records. They really knew how
to record bands then—now it's all sound reproduced by computers, no soul, no space between the musicians.

Women? It's simple: I've never had a problem.

Every encounter is sonorous. On the skin, on the lips, on the
cock. Like sediment it builds up, and the women can smell it
on you. Of course, working in the rock 'n' roll industry helps.
Like, you've been in the studio with the band for a week running, day and night, and the girlfriends, well, they start to feel
neglected. So I play this tune in my head: You-poor-little-
furry-thing-you-need-some-loving-I'm-here-for-you-I'm-here-
to-serve-every-part-of-your-delicious-body-yes-I-will.

Over and over; mantra-like. And the women, they start
quivering. Their antennae spin frantically and bend in my
direction. Before they know it they're leaning toward the mixing desk, those low, silent frequencies converging, drawing
them closer and closer. The boyfriend, the singer, disappears
into the toilets to do a line of coke. I balance the descent as she
slips me her telephone number written in lipstick on the back
of a matchbox.

Later at my place, I lay her down between the speakers, undressing her on the lounge-room floor. It's my ritual. There is a great symmetry in repetition. If I have any musical talent it is this, drawing out pleasure through the skin. A tattoo of rhythm. Of timbre.

After the crescendo, the woman lies like the hull of a ship, lit by the glowing valves of my record player. Buttocks pushing up octaves, nipples cutting through the descent. She is pinned by the music; her wings bash against the bass like a dying butterfly that has burst into color before its final fatal flight.

MACK

Quin had this thing about the female voice, the alto to be precise. Shirley Bassey, Nancy Wilson, Barbra Streisand—all were tonal pleasure for Quin. Just as some men are tit men, Quin was a voice man.

He had the weirdest record collection I'd ever seen, as well as this ancient system with *valves*, for Christ's sake! But his speakers were strawberry and cream. The edges of the acoustic space were razor sharp, especially on classical recordings: you knew where the bassoonist was sitting; it picked up the fourth violinist scratching his four o'clock beard. I'm telling you, you could hear the conductor draw breath just before his baton swished through the air.

I used to love sitting there, beer in one hand, joint in the other, just listening with the man. No women, no babies, no barking dogs, just Quin and his moldy furniture—the ultimate bachelor.

QUIN

I always leave work around five a.m., that way I avoid the white noise of this city. Discordant, man-made, eating up nature, swallowing birdsong, the wind, the percussion of rain.

I've fitted the car with mufflers and sealed the windows; it's my time capsule of tranquility. My silence. Mornings. Me and my car, we're black against the dawn. I drive over the bridge at Rozelle, past the new museum of fire towering like a huge red ghost. Every time my car accelerates over that bridge, I'm flying.

There's a moment just before sunrise when the birds stop singing, just for a second. Peace, like before the Word. I, Quin, name this moment the blue note. It's a B flat, played gently on a clarinet. I know it, I can feel it resonate in the cells of my being.

So, we're talking about the winter before last. I'd been working my guts out, sixteen hours a day for two weeks, with Taunting Tongues, an a cappella group: two bass, three tenor and ten sopranos. I'm just putting down the bass when the studio phone rings.

"Hello?"

"Hello, Adrian?"

The voice rises and quivers on the last syllable, a middle C caught between the diaphragm and the chest. Alto? Mezzo-soprano? She's treacle down the throat and I have to hear more.

"No, but keep talking."

"Who is this?" I'm holding my breath, I'm holding myself. This is the most perfect alto I've ever heard. Don't hang up, don't hang up. I want to see your mouth, your lips, your palate, the cleft under your tongue. My cock's quivering with each tonal nuance. Baby, please.

"You have a beautiful voice."

"Adrian? Is that you, you louse?"

"You have the most beautiful voice I've ever heard."

"OK, I'm hanging up."

"No you don't, not before you say something else. C'mon baby, say something."

"What's your name?"

"Quin."

"Qu-in."

"What's yours?"

"Felicity."

"Fe-li-city—as in *felicitas*, as in happiness."

She's like fingers, lubricated, tight, moving. Hitting the note with every vowel.

"Quin, are you still there?"

It's too late, I'm throbbing in rhythm with her consonants.

"Yes," I whispered, scared my breath will give me away.

"I'd like to meet you, Quin."

MACK

Yeah, July, what a shit of a month. I mean, we actually had a winter that year. Even the Japanese tourists were whining. I remember that day vividly. I was sitting there in the conference room, rolling a few numbers with what's-his-name from Virgin, when Quin comes rushing in. This in itself was enough to make me swivel round. Quin never rushes, he glides, like a bat, with those huge red ears pulsating.

"Mack," he says, "I've met this woman." I glance across at the

record executive sitting opposite, his London pallor and
Oxford accent sabotaging his snakeskin boots. I could see
from his expression he thought Quin was crazy, maybe even
homicidal. Then again, it was good dope.

"Quin, can't you see we're doing business here?"

"Yeah."

Quin throws himself onto the fun-fur couch. He takes a
deep drag of the joint and exhales into the Englishman's face.
Forty thousand dollars worth of studio time just went up in
smoke, I'm thinking.

"So is she soprano, mezzo-soprano or alto?" As if I cared, but
Quin looks dangerous, like really inspired. Always humor an
obsessive, you learn that in this industry.

"Mezzo-soprano slipping into contralto on every syllable
beginning with F. Hot, very hot."

I should have known then.

QUIN

The next morning I'm up at ten for the first time in four years.
Hair runs in the family on both sides. I need a shave. Normally
I wouldn't bother, but today I want to feel smooth, just in case.
I shake a razor blade clean of foam and slowly begin.

A beam of sunlight travels across the sink and my hands,
bouncing off the water. It gets me thinking about God, the
cosmos and the harmonics between C and C sharp. A high
electronic frequency makes me shake my head. Perhaps it's a new
frequency, one of limbo, of all those souls caught between
material and spiritual worlds. Even the very name of the shaving foam seems mystical. I forget what I'm doing and cut
myself. The thick welling of blood reminds me of my mortal-

ity. Not that I'm religious. What hope do I have with a Catholic father and a Jewish mother? I only believe in impulse. The power, the flesh. The only part of the Bible I remember is: "In the beginning was the Word, and the Word was with God, and the Word was God."

It's my personal philosophy: Being only came into existence once it had been given a tone. Naming was important, but already it had the constructs of culture imposed. *I am heard, therefore I exist.*

MACK

He told me they had their first meeting in the State Library. Sick. I mean what are you going to get up to in a large stone mausoleum? But then it is kind of kinky. All that whispering and toes under the table. I mean, hey, whatever turns you on. I know someone who even had a orgy in a deep freeze. Now that's perverse.

QUIN

I like it in here, especially in summer when the cold air off the stone hits you as you walk in from the sun. But now it's winter.

I'm waiting at a table, newspapers scattered in front of me. I am sick with nerves, like my cool has evaporated. For the first time in my life I feel, well, vulnerable. I have asked her to say my name out loud. I'd recognize that voice anywhere.

When I close my eyes now and visualize that moment, I see myself sitting there in my good blue shirt and black jeans. I'm little, like I've shrunk under the skin. Fear did this. I am frightened of rejection. All around me half-caught whispered phrases like "Sarah's graduating next year. She's pregnant, haven't you heard?" "We've got the mortgage to pay off and Tom still hasn't got a job" bounce off the walls and fall into my lap. Insidious, empty sounds.

I'm drumming my fingers, a little march of wood. A woman walks past in a tailored suit. This babe is on a mission. Tall, brunette, breasts visible under the blazer. Her high heels ricochet from wall to wall; "speak to me," taps the refrain from my fingers. She moves closer, trailing her fingers across a shelf of encyclopedias.

I can smell her perfume, fruity with an edge of spice. Speak to me, speak to me. She walks right past, oblivious. I shrink further into myself. I am a shadowy ghost-man, hazy around the edges.

"Quin?"

Music. The beating of angel wings, the sound of a fountain, heat across the throat. I swing around. A woman stands just behind me. Solid, middle-aged with a body that has made a comfortable pact with gravity. White skin, a nest of jet-black hair piled on top of her head. Everything is buried except her eyes, which are undeniably beautiful.

"Quin?"

The voice has me nodding like a somnambulist. She steps forward. Her hands, I notice, are remnants of a past glory.

"I'm Felicity."

Drowning in the last tone, I clasp her wrist with all the wisdom of a dead man.

FELICITY

He drove me back to his house. I remember pulling up outside and trying not to be disappointed. The house was a decrepit terrace with faded curtains drawn across the windows. We didn't say anything, we didn't need to. There are those rare moments when one just knows.

Suddenly I'm frightened. Here I am, standing in this dingy room with its leather couch and second-hand rug, in front of this tall, dark, young man. A total stranger. Maybe it's menopause, a flash of hormonal madness. In an instant my survival instinct shakes itself awake. I turn to leave, but then he moves, and nothing else matters.

He puts on a Shirley Bassey record and asks me to sing. I'm so nervous I think I'm going to throw up.

I haven't sung in years. I used to sing when I was in my early twenties, in a jazz club. That's when I met Adrian, my husband. Safe, secure, predictable. He's so—dry. He just doesn't excite me anymore. Actually I wonder whether he ever excited me.

Sing, Quin keeps telling me. What have I got to lose? My marriage? My dignity? Adrian would kill me if he could see me now.

I open my mouth and surprise myself with a perfect C. It fills the room like light. He closes his eyes. There's an ecstasy about him as he breathes the music through his skin, his very cells.

QUIN

She's singing my life, in tempo, underscoring it with the sadness, the loneliness, the great unspoken epic. I can't stop my body from moving. I am transported beyond the mundane. She is singing up all my dreams. All my forgotten memories. Even with my eyes closed, I can see the color of each tone: red shooting through yellow, black clashing into purple. I don't need to touch her, I could come now, just from the pitch of her voice sliding up and down the octaves.

"Keep singing," I whisper, "keep singing." I move behind her. My hands creep around her and begin to undo her high-collared blouse, button by button. Her breasts spill forward, pushed up by the bra, femininity under wraps. My long fingers reach for her nipples. Her breath falls short, but she keeps on singing.

I kneel before her, her breasts open to the air, the rest of her body covered by her long velvet dress. I cup her breasts and squeeze them together. I am a maestro. There is nothing hesitant as I take a nipple into my mouth, sucking hard, biting the blood to the surface.

We topple to the ground. She keeps her face averted, her eyes staring upward as she thrills along with the bass line. My mouth caresses her entire body. She will not look at me. She seems far away, her focus carried away by her magnificent voice. To me it feels as if the range and resonance of her voice is fusing with the extraordinary breasts that tumble to either side of her belly. I can feel her voice vibrating through her skin. The scale of her is operatic, her taste salty and Wagnerian, her smell, her sweat, the texture of her skin, an immeasurable wealth of orchestration.

"Quin, take me, take me . . ."

I lift my hand from between her thighs, her profile barely visible through her thick black bush.

"Keep singing."

I feel her welling up under my tongue, as she thrusts, out of control, like a bird flapping madly in a cage. I keep her pinned by my mouth, playing her like an instrument. She crouches, her skin shiny, lit by the valves, her lips pulled back like some majestic creature, a sphinx, an olive-skinned Madonna. She is singing the scales of an octave. She is close to screaming, but her breath comes in perfect pitch—middle C, D, E, F sharp. The carpet grates under her knees as, oblivious, she arches in a final climactic spasm. She traverses two full octaves in one glorious shriek.

The sound of her coming rips through the back of my head in streams of pure color as I ejaculate all over the rug. It is like John Cage in a thunderstorm, like wind through a forest. I've never heard an orgasm like it. All my fears, all my doubts evaporate for three glorious minutes. And I, Quin, know then why I had been put on earth.

That night I made love to her four times. By the third time, I knew I had to get those notes down before they evaporated forever. I keep a tape recorder behind the couch, ready to record the odd inspired moment.

I'll always remember it. Felicity was on her front, lips pressed against the carpet, pouting, pushed forward. She was breathing in short gasps. There was a pillow under her belly so her ass jutted up, the two pale orbs spread, her pussy glistening under the hair. Both of us were animal now. We existed beyond skin. No album notes, nothing to drag us into identity, just the heat and the smell and the sex.

I looked back over my shoulder and pressed the record button with my left toe. She never noticed a thing.

MACK

I still can't believe it. Like this chick, this housewife, spends one night with the Wolf, and that's it, bang! Her whole uni-

verse, microscopic though it may be, is upended. She goes
home, packs two suitcases and a trunk full of stuffed toys, hires
a taxi and leaves a note scrawled in crayon for her husband of
ten years. She was on a mission, I tell you. I know these
women. A man's persona is ultimately his most private territory. So what does this witch go and do? She treads all over
Quin, invading his very soul.

First it was the shoes. For ten years Quin had been wearing
the same pair of tennis shoes. Footwear, he believed, should
remain utilitarian, not decorative. An admirable sentiment, if
not a bit dated, but I respected it anyway.

Two months after moving in, that bitch had him wearing
brogues, for Christ's sake. I caught him tiptoeing down the
corridor, shoes in hand, blisters all over his feet. I figured she
must be some chick, I mean this guy had had the best of them,
you know, models, dancers, the usual band molls. For Quin to
take up shoes she had to have something special.

"Quin, what's this chick got on you?"

He nods slowly in that reptilian way of his and says,
"Music."

That's all, like a guru or some enlightened mystic. He had us
all fooled. Speaking as an old fool, I know.

Next thing he's coming to work in a suit, as if this is the
eighties or something. Listen, I've got nothing against the corporate, especially corporate money—it keeps the drugs rolling
in. But I like to keep suits in the conference room, not the studios. A tie at two a.m. makes the bands nervous.

Besides, it made Quin look like an exotic spider of the toxic
variety—not a great look. So I ask him to leave the suit at
home. He agrees but tells me that he's got no control, the needle runs haywire when she opens her mouth. Pure sound, he

tells me—like he doesn't even hear the words, just the tone of her voice.

Great, I think. He's finally cracked and we have an album to record by December. I'm telling you, at this point in history my ponytail is going gray.

Like I thought, she worked her alchemy on him. She moved in, washed the curtains, sorted out the wardrobe and even weeded the concrete courtyard, for Christ's sake. Gone were the seventies relics, the stashes of joint butts, torn beanbags, used guitar picks.

She threw out four hundred copies of *Stereosound, Audiophile* and *LA Ears.*

She dismantled his workbench and insisted that it be re-assembled in the back shed.

She even scrubbed the walls. The place lost that comfort-able nicotine-yellow hue. It made me edgy just walking in. It was so white you felt like donning shades. Not the domain of a nocturnal creature like Quin. Like luxury is not an issue here, unless you count the luxury of sinking into a worn leather couch, comfortably caved in from many a stoned drummer sinking his fat ass down into the upholstery.

Even the ceiling didn't escape the brutality of her scrubbing brush. Edwardian, Quin tells me, staring up at the exposed plaster swirls, as if he ever fucking cared before. Edwardian! I'm telling you, I felt like hanging garlic around my neck in case it was catching. Funny thing is, I never actually met her at the house. Quin used to take me around only when she was out. Not that I'm suggesting he was scared of her or anything. Just getting the various harmonics of his life in tune. Cautious bas-tard, I thought, you know how women can just throw your life into disarray. Especially if you're one of the great unwashed, unmarried brethren. You know, secretly I think I did want it to work. Like there might be hope for us all.

Then she did something that even I found hard to forgive. He'd given her access to the lounge room. The sacred listening site. Fatal mistake. I mean the shrine of sound was in there, stacked up on four milk crates, valves gleaming, turntable balancing on oxygen-free wires. Quin's very sanctum. His inner ear. See, women think that anything that's not to do with them, or that's not income-generating, is just a hobby. They don't understand or appreciate the nuances of obsession, especially when it comes to inanimate objects. Like record players. Quin told me he caught her standing over the machine, eyes gleaming like an insane lighthouse, duster at the ready. He nearly freaked, but then she turns around and says, "But how was I to know?", her voice alone sending him into a crippling paradox of lust and forgiveness.

Man, did he have it bad.

QUIN

How long? Six months. From Sydney's winter to the beginning of Sydney's summer. Six months of audio paradise.

During the day I walked around in a trance, the sound of her orgasm still echoing in my ears from the night before. It was the nearest thing I'd ever experienced to happiness. I felt myself softening under the continual stream of beautiful cadences, harmonics, arias and extended solo notes. They threaded through the house like glistening spider webs. I mean, Jesus, I became poetic. Religious even.

One morning in the bath, I decided that if God had a sound

it would be the sound of Felicity's orgasm. I'm telling you, I would have married this woman.

MACK

We had a Christmas booze-up that year, the usual orgiastic affair with the odd overdose in the back toilet. I can remember that one vividly because that was the only time I got to meet Felicity.

By now Quin had actually stopped smoking. He even told a client off for swearing—a heavy-metal singer renowned for the tattoo on his penis bearing the legend TIGER LOVES TAIL. Tiger was not amused.

Neither was I. I mean, this was business. OK, the guy could hum a perfect A, but I couldn't have him alienating my clients. But sentiment is a powerful thing. Besides, there weren't that many guys I could listen to Patti Smith with. So I decided to give him another six-month trial before firing him. That was between me and my karma.

So I'm sitting there, can of beer in one hand, joint in another, a gorgeous blonde number on my lap, listening to this really cute female country and western singer giving a feminist reading of Christmas—a deconstruction that cast the Virgin Mary as the true Messiah, Jesus Christ as the parasitic male invader and the Holy Spirit as an amorphous death wish. And I'm kinda focusing on this high concept of cunt worship. The blond babe is wriggling nicely at every mention of Christ, and the dope is cool, very cool. At that moment, Quin walks in with his mother.

At least I thought it was his mother, I mean what's a guy to assume when he sees his best mate with a short, comfortably stacked female around forty-five? So I'm leaping up, stashing the dope, brushing the coke off my beard, getting ready to give Mum a kiss on the cheek, when Quin says, "Mack, meet Felicity."

Mack, meet Felicity!

I'm struck dumb for a solid five minutes, and then this creature, this harridan that has destroyed my best friend's life, opens her mouth and says in the sweetest, juiciest pitch I've ever heard, "Mack, you're famous around our house."

And I find myself looking around for a six-foot black siren with melon breasts and a wasp waist, until she whispers again in saccharine tones, "Surely Quin's told you about me?"

Her magical voice still suspended in the air, I realized then that Quin was a marked man, possibly the new Messiah, lost to the cause. He will die for his ears. Like I said, it was great cocaine.

Three weeks later I'm locking up the studio. You know, pacing down the corridors, switching off lights, pulling shut the padded door.

Down the end I can see the lights still on in Quin's studio. Night owl, I'm thinking, and a little part of me starts hoping that perhaps he's reverting back to the lovable neurotic insomniac he once was, in his torn leather jacket and matted dreadlocks, emerging like a phoenix. You get these thoughts late at night in the studio. Maybe it's just turning forty-three, who knows.

So I walk in and there he is, bent over the desk like a possessed shaman, headphones engulfing his narrow head.

"How's it going?" I ask, but he's gone, twitching to a barely audible sound track. It's the final mix of Taunting Tongues. I

check the needles on the dials, none are over. Quin's the ultimate acrobat when it comes to balancing sound. It is then that
I notice the cassette. I lift it up and am just deciphering Quin's
black scrawl when he snatches it out of my hand. Quickly,
really quickly—and I thought he was lost to the music.

"C'mon," I say, "what's this? The unreleased final Elvis track?
Michael having sex with his monkey?"

Quin says nothing. He just sits on that cassette, man, slams
the headphones back on and points me out of there. Six
months, I'm thinking to myself. Like I own that joint.

QUIN

From beyond the headphones I can barely hear Mack's footsteps fading. Gone. Left alone. At last. I turn toward the mixing desk. It gleams in the dark. It is my control panel. My
cockpit. In here I have the agility of a Harrier fighter. I spin,
thin and powerful as my fingers dart from one track to another.
In here I am master of the universe.

I love this desk. It's the oldest in the studio, conceived of
long before digital audio technology. Hidden somewhere
behind that gleaming panel are a few glowing valves. I can feel
them through the metal. Comforting beacons of rationality,
promising real sound, not some computerized semblance of
noise. Mack thinks the desk is haunted by the ghost of an
audio engineer, electrocuted while mixing an acid-rock band
in the late sixties. I don't care. He was probably a great guy. He
must have been, if he loved my desk.

I control all.

In goes the cassette. Black and streamlined, it slots in perfectly. Machine sex, an intercourse of microchip and plastic.

The sound of Felicity's climax belts out from the huge speakers, reverberating around the padded walls. She sounds like a choir of vibrating harps. I stop the tape, rewind and play again.

I lay the track down on one channel, then play it back an octave higher and at twice the speed. The result is a rap, celestial but erotic.

Now for the strings. Carefully pushing the controls, slower, slower, I weave the sounds together, pulling up the cello. It will play behind the climax, its low, wailing tone threading through the descent. At that speed the pleasure translates as anguish. I plait the cello over the original track, creating a Greek chorus of wailing strings and human voice. Then I overlay the descant, high-speed version. I breathe a short prayer before playing it back—a prayer to instinct, to the intuitive ear, the only gift I have. It works. It is a carnal cantata. Felicity's orgasm is the eye of the storm, the tracks above and below it echoing and roaring like furious winds.

I grow hard. I am dictator. Conductor to a whole quartet of dewy-eyed, panting mezzo-sopranos, aggressive contraltos and one acquiescing falsetto.

I close my eyes and reach for the drum machine.

Nothing is sacrosanct. So I had the cassette, so I changed it. Maybe I wanted to play God. We all need to at some time in our lives. I was innocent. Like Einstein, I just wanted to improve on nature.

MACK

The next morning I come in around six. Something's bugging me about the way the speakers sound in studio two. So I'm stumbling down the corridor, hung over, with my jeans dragged over my pajamas, smelly teeth and bare feet. Times like this I wish I was married. I check into studio two, switch the lights on and activate the desk. I glance in the direction of Quin's studio.

I'm peering through my bloodshot retinas and what do I see—Quin, head slumped over the controls. Apparently lifeless. Listen, if you've handled as many overdoses as I have you go into automatic pilot. In a flash I'm in there, pulling Quin's head back by the hair, contemplating the risks of mouth-to-mouth, when the bastard wakes up with a scream. I nearly pass out with shock.

"Don't do that again, you hear me!"

"Do what?"

"Play dead like that!"

"I was sleeping for Christ's sake!"

You know, sometimes these encounters are fated. Like at that moment I felt there was some kind of weird acid flashback. Like I said, at times like this I wish I was married.

As for Quin, he was the walking dead. He just grabbed his cassette and stumbled out into the morning, his shades wrapped around that white face of his. And something goes *stop him, keep him here*. But I don't do it. I don't act on my instinct.

FELICITY

He lies face down, fully clothed. One arm is wrapped across his eyes, the other hangs off the edge of the bed. His hand twitches spasmodically and forms a fist in his sleep.

I am crouched on a chair watching him. It is eleven o'clock in the morning. I've been watching him like this for hours. My face is stiff, I can feel my mouth tighten with fury. I've been up all night.

He's been making love to a younger woman. The woman of my fears. Of soft young skin. The girl I can't be for him. Younger, foreign, who has his silence, his distance. The deception squeezes my heart. It stops me from breathing.

Anger has removed me from my body and made me into a different woman.

I move silently across the floor. I have license to do anything. I gently lift his arm away from his face. He smiles in his sleep.

Traitor, serpent, betrayer.

I will not be treated like this. His face is soft with sex, a half-smile twitches as he dreams.

QUIN

In a strange way I can imagine what she must have been thinking, sitting there. Love does that, it makes you one person, one mind. I see her lifting the flowered pillow and pressing it down over my face. My neck suffuses with blood, turns black-red. My arms flail blindly as I fight for my life. She presses down harder, holding on with all the strength of her anger. A super-human strength, the collective venom of generations of deceived women. Felicity is taking revenge. For fear. For jealousy. For the Fool. I see myself falling back, legs limp, fist rolling open, lifeless. In Felicity's mind. But I cannot reach her because I am asleep, struggling blindly with my dreams. Sensing her there beyond a cloud of crackling static. Turning on the bed, I believe I am safe.

FELICITY

Standing over him, watching him, his breath sour-sweet, cigarettes and hash, the hair on his chest curling defiantly, I find I
still want him. Want him more with the strangeness, the lust of
another.

I want to slip my hand under the bedcovers to find his warm
penis. He would be half-erect, still damp, fragrant with
strange. I stand there paralyzed, debating my next move. My
eyes move over the disheveled terrain of his body. His leather
jacket is spread across his feet like a faithful dog. The cassette
is half hanging out of the red silk-lined pocket. I reach for it.

The valves flicker for a second and slowly begin to glow. The
needles on the dials escalate wildly for a moment, then settle
down to mid-point as I adjust the volume. He still sleeps
upstairs. I don't want to wake him.

I sit down carefully on the battered leather couch and place
the headphones over my ears. The leads spiral down like
deranged umbilical cords. I am terrified. Frightened my suspi-
cions will be confirmed in an avalanche of evidence. My hand
shakes as I push the play button. The orchestrated sound of a
woman's orgasm sweeps through me. A tidal wave of groans,
grunts and breath. For a moment I am swept along by the sheer
majesty of this human cacophony. I forget myself. I am rolling
naked in a landscape of tongues, of lips, of taut skin, on the
borderline of pleasure and pain, the music sweating beads of
ecstasy. I become wet, I can't help myself. Quin dances before
me, a whirling dervish with a lithe, naked succubus wound
around his sweating buttocks. By the first crescendo he is
above her, entering her, filling her. *Sotto voce* and he is buried
between her legs, drawing from this witch the sweetest of

notes. One minute it is red hair that is thrown across a white back, next minute it is shorn pale blond pressed up against a full bruised mouth. Nowhere do I find myself. This voice is not mine. Nor this body, that can bend in one smooth descending octave.

I stand over the stove. Bubbles rise in the boiling oil, burst and then course through the thick liquid. I am there and I am not there. It isn't my hand pouring the boiling oil into the turkey baster, it isn't my trembling fingers struggling with the plunger of the icing-sugar syringe.

Still deeply asleep, his head lolls as I prop him up. Carefully tilting his face, I insert the turkey baster into his left ear, then the end of the icing-sugar syringe into his right. There is no doubt in my mind, just the cry of that orgasm, the sound of the woman who betrayed us echoing again and again. I squeeze.

QUIN

People think deafness is a sound. It's not. It's snow, static snow. A constant blizzard in the back of the head. An ice age of silence. I am a polar bear stumbling through shards of frost.

I see Mack waving from the other side of a frozen lake. He is trying to tell me that he loves me, that he still wants me to work for him even if I'm totally deaf. I swing my heavy neck and look back toward the blinding white terrain that stretches into infinity. Polar bears are solitary creatures.

Two men. One, large, on the brink of middle-age, leans against an open window. Outside the afternoon traffic rattles past, sending up clouds of dust into the sunlight that cuts into the dingy lounge room. He pushes back his thinning hair and lights another cigarette.

The second man crouches by a record player, his long arms wrapped around his knees. He rocks himself backward and forward to the vibrations he can feel through the worn floorboards. He knows that the room is filled with the sound of a woman's orgasm. Her cries fuse with the violins, bounce off the high plaster ceiling and pour out onto the street.

Pomegranate

The house has white Grecian pillars and a small front yard with a pomegranate tree. I was attracted to it because of the tree; I remembered that pomegranates symbolize fertility. When Adrian heard that he said, "Sweetheart, we have to have it." Before we moved we had an apartment in the city, one of those thirties places, all white plaster and curved balconies. It was beautiful, except for the constant sound of traffic throughout the day, then at night the transport trucks would start up. I'd lie there imagining it was the sea, but it didn't work. I'd wind up tighter and tighter, my jaw clenched, muscles aching with exhaustion. Adrian said that's why the baby thing wasn't working. He thinks eggs and spermatozoa need sunshine and peace. Otherwise we'd end up conceiving an insomniac and that would be worse than no kid at all.

Adrian is a senior accountant. I have a job at Belle's Beauty Parlor, along the highway. I do facials, bikini waxes and the odd pedicure.

From where I sit I can see the long backyard with two rows of citrus trees planted to hide the back fence. If I turn around I face the door of the veranda and our newly renovated open-plan kitchen and dining area. I feel safe here and sort of ripe, like a pomegranate—when its skin splits open you can see all the juicy red seeds bursting to get out. When we first moved in I painted the small bedroom pink, then drew a mural of cartoon characters around the border. Adrian hated it. He thinks children shouldn't be spoilt. But then Adrian was brought up in a poky little house with linoleum floors and a gas fire while his mother slaved her guts out to send him to boarding school, sometime in the fifties, long before I was even born.

I painted the house six months ago and I'm still not pregnant. We've done all the things we're meant to do. I've got a fertility chart pinned up on the fridge: red for ovulation, pink for just before and orange is time out.

It's great, except that Adrian is color-blind and sometimes mistakes orange for red. When we first started it was kind of sexy, like tightrope walking without a net. Adrian got really scared. He said it reminded him of his own mortality. He thinks a lot about his own death. I don't, I think a lot about giving birth, and feeling the tug of the baby's lips on my nipples. Sometimes I have this fantasy when I'm trying to get to sleep. I travel down my own bloodstream, imagining that I'm an egg, all fat and juicy, just being released from the ovary. I'm floating along the fallopian tube, bouncing gently against the soft, spongy walls feeling really relaxed and really horny when along comes this sperm, its tail swishing behind it like a long whip. It stops and sniffs and comes plunging straight for me with this really determined look on its face. I reel back as it burrows into my side. I usually have an orgasm then. The trouble is none of the sperm look like Adrian. They all look like film stars or rock singers or ex-boyfriends.

Afterward, when I open my eyes, I feel ever so slightly

guilty. I look across at Adrian, his great cliff of a chin pointing up towards the ceiling, those slightly bulging eyes closed and twitching in his sleep, and I think, fuck it, it's not as if they can get into your head, is it?

I've explored most of the house, except the attic. I went up the ladder once but I got frightened. When I was a kid we used to go on expeditions up in our attic. My brother would lead the way, pretending he was a great explorer, picking his way carefully over the ceiling beams and over great wads of insulation material. Dad had told us that if we stepped between the beams we'd fall through the ceiling and back into the house. All the history of our parents' marriage was packed up there: photos, a moldy piece of wedding cake, an old plastic breast pump of my mother's that we thought was a piece of obscene torture equipment. I stole some of the cake once and kept it for years in a locket for good luck. It went green.

My father left when I was seven. It destroyed my mom. Being Catholic, she was too ashamed to demand a divorce. I haven't seen him since. I think they're still married. After he left I refused to go up into attics anymore.

Adrian's been up into ours. He said it was small and dirty. He brought down a small, battered leather suitcase. Inside was an ancient wedding dress. It looked like a 1920s design, with seed pearls sewn into the neckline. There was even a tiny crown of flowers, woven around a tiara of cut glass. Adrian wanted to sell it. But I'm superstitious, so I had the dress dry-cleaned, folded it up with mothballs and packed it into the bottom of a cupboard.

We've been married for three years. Since I was twenty-one and Adrian was thirty-nine. I had to play all sorts of games to get him to marry me. I don't believe in people just living together—the girl's got no security. It wasn't easy, I tell you, this being Adrian's second marriage and all. Still, I got him in the end.

I haven't really had a lot of men. Actually only four and a half. The first was Robin. We never did it until right at the end, mostly we just kissed and touched a lot. Mom brought us up to believe that sex was a spiritual and holy act. I believed that right up until I was eighteen. Then I had my first orgasm and thought I saw God.

We were in the mountains. It was just after the end-of-year exams. Robin had told his father he was going down the coast with a few surfing mates and I'd told Mom I was going to spend a night at my best friend's parents' holiday house. That part was sort of true, I mean I *was* at Anne's house, but her parents were away in Europe and it was just me and Robin and Anne and her boyfriend.

I'd lied to Anne and had told her that Robin and I had been screwing for months. So she'd put us in a bedroom of our own. It overlooked a gully and had windows from the ceiling to the floor, with no curtains. Anne's father was an architect and he'd designed the house so that the surrounding forest seemed to grow right into it—leaves curled in through the windows and around the arched balconies.

Robin and I had spent the night naked, lying wrapped around each other, both of us touching and caressing until the early morning. I remember staring out watching the moon fade into the sky. Then, as the bellbirds began echoing across the valley, I fell asleep.

I was woken by this delicious feeling. There had been a bar of chocolate beside the bed and Robin was running the melted chocolate down from my belly button. It tickled, I laughed,

Robin looked up at me. His concentration was intense. Crouching by my side he placed a hand between my legs. I resisted, then shyly let him push my thighs wide apart. He sat there, kneeling between my open legs gazing down at me in wonder. He traced the chocolate across my belly and down towards my pussy. Carefully he ran the chocolate across my lips, barely touching me, the lightest of caresses flicking across my clit. I groaned and tried to move away, but his arms held me down. He gently pushed the bar into me, the chocolate was warm and trickled down. He moved it backward and forward, lubricating me. Then pulling it out, he slowly ran his tongue along the path of the chocolate, around and into my belly button, down the center of my stomach, then, still holding me wide apart, started to lick the inside of my thighs. I'm twisting and groaning and thrashing around in pleasure. His tongue licking everywhere but where I wanted it to be. Slowly he moved toward my clit. Flicking it lightly with his tongue, then fastening onto it with his mouth, sucking hard. I started to shake with excitement. I was out of control. I pulled Robin up by the hair. His sex nudged against me, the tip of it just resting inside. He slid in, it didn't hurt, I was well prepared, but the size and shape of it filled me in a way I had never imagined. He rolled over and pulled me up over him, so that I was sitting above him. Instinctively, I started to slide up and down his cock. I felt like I was being impaled every time he slid into me. It hurt slightly but the pleasure made me forget the pain.

I remember looking across the dawn sky as I rode him. The bed was right against the window and I felt as if I was riding into the sunrise like some mythical figure. The sun had begun to fill the sky with a rosy light. My pleasure grew with the flooding light. The more furiously I rode, the higher the sun rose. I felt as if I was in control of the sky, that if I stopped the sun would drop back behind the earth and all would sink back into darkness. Soon I could feel the ripples of intense pleasure contracting upward. As I screamed in the throes of my first orgasm I thought I saw a translucent bluish shadow race across the huge red orb of the sun. At the time I thought I had seen God. I know now that I *did* see something, because I've seen other things since.

Last night was amazing! I didn't think Adrian could perform like that. Not that he's a lousy lover or anything. Far from it, I mean for his age he's incredible. He's even had a second erection on a couple of occasions. But last night was truly unbelieveable!

I still can't believe it, so I'll get it down in writing. Adrian came in late after a board meeting. I'd prepared his favorite dish, spaghetti marinara. We ate in silence. I tried making conversation but Adrian was too tired to respond.

"Honeybun, do you like the meal?"

"Too much tomato." He reaches across for the cheese and sprinkles copious amounts onto his plate. I pretend not to notice. I wish he'd say something, anything to let me into his day. He picks up the business section of the paper.

"Dollar's down again. Damn Wayne!"

"What's Wayne done?"

"Told me to buy Ampol. They've dropped four points."

"Fascinating, darling." A party starts up next door and I wonder about all those warnings my friends gave me about marrying an older man.

"I'm off to bed."

"But it's only nine o'clock. Do you know what day it is?"

"No, I haven't had a chance to look at the damned schedule, Jodie."

"It's a red day. And there's no need to get aggressive."

"I am not getting aggressive! I'm just exhausted. Besides, I've got to be in at seven-thirty tomorrow morning. Head office has called an emergency meeting."

"Don't you want to have a child?"

"Yes, but not tonight." There are bags under his eyes, and his hairline seems to have receded further despite the implants. I kiss him, but he tastes bitter. " 'Night, love. I'll sit up for a while."

He plods heavily along the corridor as I switch on the television. The party next door thumps through the wall. I haven't been to a party in ages. The last one was Adrian's office Christmas party and I was the youngest there by ten years. I get up and dance for a few minutes by myself in the center of the room. I imagine that there is a young dark man leaning into me. He has his knee between my legs and we're dancing really close. I can smell his thick black hair and his aftershave. He grips my buttocks with his hands as he bites into my neck. He has slicked-back hair and elegant Mediterranean features. I trip over the remote control and knock my head on the side of the sofa. I lie there for a moment, dazed. I can smell the vague scent of aftershave drifting in from the open window. It must be from the party.

Later I go to bed. Adrian is sleeping on his side. The music is still going on next door. I'm wearing the silk nightgown Adrian gave me for my twenty-fourth birthday, hoping that the feel of the silk will inspire him to take me suddenly in the middle of all this thumping darkness.

I lie on my back, staring up at the ceiling. The wind outside blows the gate shut with a bang. I shiver and turn on my side.

The smell of aftershave drifts in again. In my half sleep I see a seascape. A tiny bay, untouched by civilization. The clear blue waves creep up the pale sand; the wind brings the smell of cyprus and eucalyptus across my face. I open my eyes with a jolt. The scent of heat and the trees still lingers in the room.

The room has grown darker, and the party next door is over. In the distance the last guest pulls away from the curb.

The room is jet black. I feel his hands move under the silk. They run down my back and creep around to my breasts. I lie there waiting for his usual move, which is to roll me toward him. Instead, he runs his tongue down the length of my spine. Parting my buttocks he works his way around to my vagina with his mouth, caressing me with his tongue. He hoists himself up through my open legs so that he lies facing me.

My lover is completely silent. His hands feel altered, changed. I can barely see his profile. His eyes are shut, his lips are pulled back in a strange grimace. He takes my hands roughly with one hand and pins them back against the pillow. With the other hand he squeezes my breasts together. His skin is unusually coarse. He smells different, there is musk on his neck. I find myself trying to remember what I washed his shirt in the day before. He lifts my legs high up above his shoulders, holding me open by spreading my thighs. He plunges into me. His violence is infectious. He grasps my buttocks with both hands. He has me pinned. In the darkness I feel as if there are fingers in every orifice, probing, opening me up. We climax together. It is a first.

I made a huge breakfast this morning, all Adrian's favorites— bacon, eggs and American flapjacks. He just sat there and asked what the occasion was.

"Don't tease me." I kissed him on the ear.

He pushed me away and said, "Really. I don't know."

"You know, last night."

"What about last night?"

"You were pretty damned fantastic, that's what."

"Was I?"

I kissed his other ear. You know, sometimes he can be really cute, the way he plays games. He went really quiet and didn't even finish his flapjacks. Male menopause. It makes them so unpredictable. If he doesn't want to talk about it that's his prerogative. He's funny about talking about his emotions. It's because of Felicity, his first wife. She was a failed jazz singer and an amateur social worker, and she got him to talk about everything. Even when there wasn't a problem. He hated that. Adrian says that what you see is what you get. He thinks people invent trouble for themselves. He's a pragmatist, my Adrian. That's why I haven't told him about some thing—you know, like my second sight. He wouldn't understand.

That afternoon, I was just in the middle of putting on a customer's clay face pack when an image suddenly came into my mind from the night before. Adrian's hand in the dark. I had the definite impression that he was wearing a signet ring on his little finger. And I'm sure it had a ruby in it. The more I stood there with this vision in my head, the more convinced I was. I even let the mask dry over the customer's mouth by accident. The strange thing is that Adrian doesn't wear a signet ring, and we made love in total darkness. Maybe it's because I'm all shook up and jittery today. I hope it's hormonal. I hope it's because the chart worked and I conceived.

I found an old war medal behind the chest of drawers later that week. It was made of copper with an embossed boar's head on it. Adrian thinks it's from Sicily, from the Second World War. I remember our neighbor telling me that there used to be an old Italian living here before us, that he died in the house. I guess the medal must have belonged to him. I put it in with the wedding dress.

Last night was weird again. I'm getting ready for bed, when he suddenly appears behind me. Strange because I've just left him in the study watching TV. So there he is, close enough to feel his breath on my shoulder, and he asks me in this deep voice to put on my corset. The one we used at the beginning, for fun. He's got this look in his eyes which means business, so I slip it on and add black stockings for effect, but no underpants. He tells me to lie on the bed. Again I feel as if I'm with a stranger. As if all the familiarity, scent, gesture, even the way he walks toward me, is foreign. I lie down on the bed and he turns the lamp so that it's shining fully down onto my crotch. He reaches under the bed and pulls out a small bowl full of hot water, an old fashioned shaving brush and a razor.

"What are you doing?"

"I want you clean, like a young girl."

Shadows fall across the wall, and for a moment I don't recognize the short black figure crouching over my slender form. He begins to soap me up. Foam covers my cunt. Carefully, with the precision of a doctor, he scrapes the hair off with the razor. Over the top toward my sex mouth, strips of wispy blond hair fall away. I watch fascinated, feeling the air across my newfound nakedness. Then hoisting me up with the help of a pillow, he begins to work on the outer lips, transforming them into virginal pink innocence. The shape of me emerging like a seashell, the ripples, the contours, the ridge of my clitoris rising undeniably. The heat of the lamp turning my thighs rosy.

He stands just inches away from my face. Staring into his eyes I am hypnotized. There is that smell of aftershave again. He drops to the floor, his face hidden. He runs his hands up my legs, between my lips. I can feel his breath as he blows gently. He moves my legs farther apart. He looks down at me, his eyes burning holes through my body. "Look," he says and holds the mirror up so I can see myself. Pink, innocent, naked, I glisten like a split peach. *"Che bella, bellissima Madonna,"* he says.

Shocked, I freeze. This isn't his voice. This isn't Adrian. "Kneel," he says. I kneel over his face. My breasts fall heavily out of the corset. He takes me into his mouth, licking furiously. I am just about to come when he sits up and swings me over his knee and begins to spank me hard, the sound of each slap echoing around the bedroom. I try to move away but he has me firmly gripped between his knees. The heat from each spank rises up in between each smack.

"You're hurting me!"

"Che?"

"Adrian, you're hurting me!" I feel my flesh redden and grow hot. It begins to turn me on. I want him inside me. I ask him please, now. Do it now! He stops and listens. My voice is suddenly gigantic in the silence.

Slowly he enters me. He feels larger inside me, different. We come together for the second time.

The next morning I found an old letter when vacuuming around the couch. It was neatly folded and tied with a red ribbon. There was something familiar about the way it smelled. The letter was written in a spindly female hand. At first I thought it was French, but then I recognized some of the words as Italian. I slipped it into my pocket, as I was running late for work.

It was only later when I was having a coffee with Gina that I remembered the letter. She was able to translate it for me.

16 July 1942

My darling Alberto,

You have been gone for over six months and I am beginning to forget the sound of your voice. The house is looking beautiful, especially the pome-granate you planted over the front porch. They have no winter here and the sun is like down south, always on the back of your neck. Yesterday your mother brought over some plums she grew herself. She told me not to listen to the Australians. That as an Italian you have the right to fight for who you believe in. It's easier at work. I think the women have forgotten that you exist!

Harry, the foreman, gave me a copy of Il Actione! He'd found it in the men's section. I read it from cover to cover. It even smelled of Sicily! I miss you Alberto. Please come home soon.

All my love
Leonie

I folded up the letter and put it in with the old wedding dress and medal that lay carefully wrapped in a box at the bottom of the cupboard. Somehow I felt that it belonged there.

I got my period today. I suppose it was predictable, but I had convinced myself that this time I really was pregnant. I'd had all the signs: my breasts were aching and swollen, and I'd even had a slight discharge. So when I saw the blood on the sheets I was filled with a heavy despair. Adrian didn't help. He

shouted at me this morning for using his razor. At the time I
was too distressed by the blood on my thighs to answer him.
Anyway, I don't even shave my legs—I get them waxed for free
at the salon. I put it down to work stress, it's the end of the tax
year. Adrian's gone crazy, he's obsessed with the idea of paying
off the mortgage early. After he left, I happened to glance at
the razor. There were tiny flecks of black hair stuck in the
blade. I'm a natural blonde, and Adrian is a redhead, or he was
before he started going bald. It's a mystery.

I spoke to our neighbors yesterday. Mrs. Harris has been living next door for the past twenty years. She knew Mr. Alberto
Mantilli really well. She thinks the letter might have been from
his wife. She died long before Mrs. Harris's time and old
Alberto never talked about her. I wonder if Adrian would go
silent like that if I died. Recently I've been wondering whether
he loves me at all. He never says it, you know, the words. I
used to pass it off as typical Anglo-Saxon behavior, that maybe
he just hadn't had the training to express his love for me. Now
I don't know.

He's gone away on a two-day conference in Canberra. Last
night I went out to a South American bar with Gina and Mary
from the salon. It was great—free drinks for the ladies and a
fantastic band playing calypso music. Mary got talking to this
really handsome boy from Colombia while I danced with his
brother. He looked about sixteen, although he told me he was
twenty-three. It was great flirting and later he told me I was
beautiful.

By the time I got home I was drunk. Not real drunk but
drunk enough to forget that Adrian had gone away. I stumbled
out of the taxi and down the garden path. The pomegranate
loomed over the front porch. It looked far larger than the

scraggly little thing Adrian had nearly pruned to death earlier that summer.

I finally managed to fit the key into the lock, once inside I noticed the corridor light shining. In my drunken haze I assumed that Adrian had left it on for me. The kitchen light was on too. I'd only eaten a couple of peanuts that night, so I was starving. There was a smell of cooking, something I didn't recognize. I thought that maybe Adrian had left a container of take-out food in the microwave, but it was empty. I made myself some toast and honey, and ate it quickly to stop the room from spinning. I realized I wasn't going to make it to the bedroom so I lay down on the couch.

I open my eyes and look down at my body. Under a long, old-fashioned white linen dress is my belly. Swollen, pregnant. I run my hands over my body—I am large. I shift my weight, feeling the baby press against my lower organs. My bladder feels tight. I am so happy, I want to cry out to Adrian to tell him. I sit up, and feel long hair fly back over my shoulders. I look down—it is black hair, long black hair. Terrified, I stand up, the sudden weight of my womb sending me stumbling against the couch. The carpet has changed to an old-fashioned floral. As I fall, I realize that the room has no sound. No echo. I'm dreaming, I think, and shut my eyes, trying to wake up. I open them again, but nothing has changed. My belly pro- trudes in front of me. My feet, normally small with tiny toes, are not my own. I walk soundlessly toward the bathroom. It is behind the same door, but the white tiles Adrian and I put in have been replaced by old-fashioned green ones, and the shower unit has been replaced by a huge white enamel bath. There is no sink—only an old tin baby's bath propped up against the cracked wall. I lean over and pick up an oval shaving mirror that hangs off a bare hook.

My hands shake as I lift it up toward my face. Staring back from the mirror is a completely alien face. I scream. I mean, my mouth opens and I scream, but no sound comes out. I lift the mirror again. She is in her early thirties, with a long angular face, high cheekbones and deep-set brown eyes. Long black hair frames her face. It is the eyes that terrify me. They are full of pain and sadness, but totally vacant. They are the eyes of a dead person.

The next day I had a terrible hangover, not to mention a neckache from sleeping with my head pushed up against the arm of the couch. I glanced at my watch and realized I was an hour late for work. I didn't remember my dream until much later at the parlor, when I noticed that a long black hair had wound itself around my wedding ring.

I found another letter the day after Adrian got back from Canberra. This one was in English. Bad English. It hadn't been sent. It was tucked behind the bathroom cabinet and the wall, all folded up as if someone had left it there for me to find. I think it was from the woman, the one in my dream. I think she was Mr. Mantilli's dead wife. I don't know why, but I hid the letter from Adrian. Before I'd even opened it. I knew immediately that he mustn't ever see the letters. I guess I thought he'd never understand, like the way I could never tell him that I saw things. Knowing Adrian he'd probably send me to a shrink or ban me from drinking with Gina.

I waited until he left for work and then I opened it. It was on expensive paper that had yellowed with age. A mold stain covered a quarter of it, but the spidery writing was still visible underneath.

13 August 1942

Mi darlin Harry,

I love yu, truelly I do. But I donta think we meet in the park by the ponda no more. People are talkin an their mouths are cruel.

Please understand mi love.

Leonie

The letter really depressed me. I hid it in an old make-up box I keep in my underwear drawer.

When Adrian came back from Canberra he seemed to have reverted back to his normal self—you know, tired every night, obsessive about the crossword, worried about money. Then gradually, after two days, a change came over him. Chicken cacciatore on Tuesday. Fettuccine puttanesca on Wednesday. He's a meat-and-two-veg man from way back. I started to really worry.

Then on Friday, after watching a late-night western, Adrian opens his briefcase and brings out a riding crop.

"What's that for?"

"Fun."

"What kind of fun?"

"You'll see." He starts swishing it through the air with this strange grin on his face. I'm starting to think that maybe I should confront him about his behavior. I mean how weird is weird? Then I remember that it's a pink day.

"You're not going to hurt me with that, are you?"

"I'll be gentle, I promise."

Kneeling in front of the TV, he kisses me on the lips and leads me into the bedroom. He makes me lie on the bed front forward while he pushes up my skirt. He ties my ankles to the headboard and stuffs pillows under my thighs to push my ass higher. Then he binds my hands together and suspends the rope from the light fixture in the ceiling.

My torso is now lifted up from the bed, my legs spread-eagled. He slowly unfastens the small pearl buttons of my blouse, revealing my cleavage. He works over me in silence; it is like I'm with a stranger, his hands alien on my skin.

He runs the end of the riding crop down the inside of my thighs, flicking up the back of my skirt, and slowly rolls my panties down as far as they will go. The plaited end of the riding crop trails across my buttocks. I clench involuntarily, imagining the welts across my unmarked skin. My heart has begun to beat high up in my throat, but I can feel myself grow moist. I don't want him to see my wetness. I don't want to let him into my pleasure. In a mirror, I can see that I am beautiful like this, my torso pulled upward, my breasts pushed up between my raised arms, like a picture of a saint from a catechism book I had as a kid.

I don't recognize the way he is moving around the bed, his step so controlled, as if he knows exactly what he's doing—so different from his usual clumsiness.

I close my eyes. I can feel the blind head of his penis as he trails it up the back of my legs, starting at the sole of my left foot, nudging for a moment against the hollow of my toes, then up, up the back of my calf, barely brushing the skin, and up the inside of my thigh. He stops just before the flesh dips into the Mount of Venus. My clitoris is pushed against my panties, which are pulled tight into my damp crotch.

I can feel the gush of air as he brings the riding crop down sharply across my buttocks. I gasp, the pain a map of vibration across my skin. Then a numbness floods in as he strikes, again and again and again. I lose count. The blood rushing to the surface brings with it an incredible heat.

He stops and I lie there, throbbing. Something cold and wet is poured over my skin. Slowly it slips across my back leaving a sensation of soothing whiteness in its path. He rubs the cold olive oil down between my cheeks, spreads my lips and runs his oily fingers over them.

He then sits over me, kneeling between my thighs, and fucks me violently, his fingers tugging at my clitoris as he slides in and out, the cold oil trickling all the way into my womb, cooling my insides as it oozes between the skin of his cock and my cunt.

I stare into the mirror, but Adrian's reflection is cut off at the neck. I watch the movement of his buttocks as he slides in and out. A shadow is thrown by candlelight across the back wall, and I stare as he throws back his face, his profile etched clearly against the stippled white wallpaper. But the shadow is wrong—this isn't Adrian's nose, this isn't Adrian's chin. And something inside of me crystallizes in shock.

Sitting alone the next day I started to panic. I couldn't tell whether I was imagining or seeing things. I decided to cook and clean the house—it's my way of dealing with anxiety. The girls at work always know when I'm nervous because I'll spend twice as long making sure that every last hair is pulled out of the client's legs. After gathering up all the sheets and putting them into the washing machine I started to prepare a casserole.

Anything to make things normal between us again. In the middle of chopping up the beef I realized that I'd run out of paprika.

Mrs. Harris let me into that dark front room of hers, with the fifties furniture and old rugs. There was an older woman sitting with her back to me, staring absentmindedly out at the overgrown garden visible through the French doors. I couldn't help noticing the way she was crumbling a biscuit into her tea. Neurotic.

"Jodie, this is Maude Billinger, she's from number six. Jodie's from number nine. Mrs. M!" Maude was obviously deaf, but she swung around at the mention of number nine.

"I know that house."

"Jodie was asking about Mr. Mantilli. Remember him, dear?"

"What?"

"Alberto Mantilli!"

"There's no need to yell, I'm not a half-wit! Of course I remember Alberto, his wife Leonie used to make dresses for the girls. Lovely woman. Beautiful too."

I leaned forward, not wanting to betray too much curiosity in my voice. "What happened?"

"What do you mean, love?"

"Why did she disappear?" Maude and Mrs. Harris exchanged glances. Maude gestured vaguely toward the garden.

"What harm can the truth do? They're all off with the angels now." Maude looked carefully at me as she spoke. She had a narrow face, with a web of heavy wrinkles around clear green eyes. She must have been beautiful once herself.

"She didn't disappear, love. She died, just after Alberto got back." Mrs. Harris, now keen, moved forward dramatically.

"He was in the war, you know, fighting for the other side. Oh, it was a terrible scandal around here."

"The other side?"

"The fascists, love."

"That's beside the point. Trouble was, by the time he got back Leonie was pregnant . . ."

". . . but not by him, see."

I was reeling now. I remembered staring into the bathroom mirror, my black eyes full of pain, my belly swollen under my white tunic. I didn't want to know anything else. But the two old women were insistent, the truth must be told.

"Harry Whittle, that's who the culprit was."

"A bit of a lad, was Harry, a smooth talker. He always got the ladies in."

"Poor Leonie. Not talking the lingo, she thought he was for real but when Alberto got home . . ."

"It was terrible!"

"You're not wrong there, it was gossip for years afterward."

I couldn't hold back. "What happened?"

"Well, Alberto had only been back a day and . . ."

"She tried to get rid of the baby, you know, the ignorant way."

"Alberto found her in the bathroom."

"He came out of the house with her in his arms, screaming he was."

"I remember the way her hair was hanging down. She had beautiful long black hair."

"She bled to death, poor thing, never had a chance. Alberto grieved for months. See, he loved her. He would have had her. Child and all."

"So he said, after the event. Men are like that, afterward."

Leonie. I had dreamt through her eyes. My womb had become hers. I went back into the house clutching Mrs. Harris's paprika, my stomach heaving.

Adrian was waiting for me, naked with just the bath towel wrapped around his waist. He held the dripping bath soap in his right hand. "What's the meaning of this?" He held out the yellow cube. Long black pubic hairs were stuck to it.

"They're not mine."

"I can see that."

"Adrian, I haven't got a lover."

"Then how did they get there?"

"I don't know!" He swung back into the bathroom and slammed the door. The mirror in the lounge room rattled with the crash.

I gazed into the pot of stew, and shook in the paprika. It descended like red snow, settling onto the thick bubbling gravy. Leonie Mantilli must have been at least four months pregnant. A pain shot across the front of my womb, making me fall against the stove.

Adrian is silent over the meal. He picks through the casserole like he is picking over a corpse. I want to tell him about the Mantillis, I want to tell him about the first time I saw some one from the other side. But as I form sentences in my mind I falter. Adrian is a fact man, he can only deal with reality. He puts his fork down.

"It's the same man who used my razor, isn't it?"

"Adrian, I am not having an affair."

"Was he over here when I went to Canberra? Is that your little arrangement?"

"Please believe me, I am not having an affair!"

"Then how do you explain the hair and the grease!?"

"What grease?"

"I found some kind of disgusting pomade all over my comb,

and it certainly wasn't mine. Or have you taken to using Bryl-creem recently?"

"Look, this is going to sound really stupid . . ." I ventured.

"Try me."

"It's a ghost. I think this house is haunted."

"That is pathetic, Jodie. Surely you can come up with a better story than that!"

He storms out, his plate crashing down to the floor as he leaves. I sit staring into my glass of wine. It looks so cool and calm in there, if only I could just dive in. Outside there is the sound of his car starting up. I don't want to be left alone. I don't want to be left alone in this house.

I sit naked on the edge of the bed. I tell myself my name is Jodie. I run my hands through my hair, my shoulder-length blond hair. I trace the planes of my face, feeling the bridge of my short nose which disappears into the full curves of my cheeks. I press the palms of my hands against my breasts, feeling their weight, feeling them sitting high on my chest. I clutch at my abdomen. I know that my womb is empty.

Something moves in the shadows. I freeze. Only my eyes shift, peering into the dark recesses. A man stands by the bedroom door. He is short and dark, his eyes a warm brown in the greenish shadow, his hair a shining helmet. He is in his late thirties, and is wearing an old-fashioned suit with a crisp white shirt peering above a waistcoat. He is holding a battered leather suitcase in one hand and a Trilby hat in the other. He winks at me, a languid batting of the eyelid, then smiles, the arch of white teeth splitting his tanned face.

I swing around. Adrian stands there looking sheepish. "I drove around for hours before I realized I had no place else to go."

I hug him. His body, resistant, eventually softens against mine. His hands creep up to my breasts. We fall onto the bed. Frantically I pull his shirt free and undo his trousers. I bury my face in the fur of his testicles, his penis, still soft, rolls across my cheeks. He smells fantastic. I take him into my mouth, feeling him grow hard. He pulls me up to his lips and we kiss. His tongue traces the inside of my lips. He sucks my tongue as if I am the man and he is the woman.

My ankles are resting on his shoulders as he holds my calves and pushes my legs even farther apart. He plunges into me. I feel my whole body rotating around the swollen head of his cock, savoring every grain of his skin as he slowly slides in and out. Someone is sucking on my clit. I crane my neck to see if Adrian is touching me, but his hands are firmly around my ankles. I gasp—a tongue is slowly caressing the tip and then sucking hard on the tiny shaft. I am delirious with pleasure. It isn't rational, nothing is touching me there, and yet I can feel a man's breath blowing across my hips, his lips over me, as Adrian's cock gains rhythm. Paroxyms of bliss tear through my belly. I am coming, contracting wildly. The scream of my orgasm breaks out from my throat, and it echoes in the dark.

He lies with his back to me, curled up against the hollow of my belly. I am staring out at the wall, my mind skipping backward and forward in waves.

I remember the figure I saw against the sky that morning with Robin in the mountains.

I see red streaming down my thighs. I see a bathtub full of blood.

My lover stirs. *"Leonie, sono a casa."*

And I find myself replying, *"Si, Alberto, si."*

ICE CREAM

The long old-fashioned bus gleams a steel gray in the sunshine as it waits outside the red brick gates of the school. Cicadas echo shrilly in the summer afternoon. The fifties fender painted scarlet and blue runs the whole length of the bus. Above the grid of the radiator sits a tiny statue of a silver ballerina. Tinkerbell, the little girls call her. One side of the bus is opened up to display the tubs of ice cream sitting just out of arm's reach.

Above the advertisements for double-chocolate whips, vanilla scoops with raspberry, and choc-and-nut supremes is a hand-painted sign embellished with dancing clowns and luminous red balloons: Jerome's homemade ice cream, the finest in Illinois. Underneath, visible through the two windows flanking the open hatch is Jerome himself, busy filling up huge plastic containers of ice cream, ready for the three o'clock rush.

Jerome lifts the large silver trowel and digs it into the freezer of ice cream. It sinks with a crunch. He, cooled by the air lifting up from the open freezer, transfers the ice cream into the plastic container sitting just below the counter. His arms, muscular and tanned, strain against his thin cotton T-shirt as he

lifts the heavy scoop. His neck, strong and sculpted, rises up
from the swelling curves of his shoulders. His chest hair etches
a black wispy pattern between the cushions of his breasts and
over his white T-shirt. Beads of sweat hang suspended,
momentarily arrested by the gusts of frozen air. Bent sideways
in concentration, Jerome reveals small ears set closely against
his skull. The translucent perimeters are flushed deep red with
the heat. If you traveled across from his ears, you would find
yourself walking up the steep incline of his cheekbones. Two
jutting mountains, delicate in strength, perhaps betraying
some past Mongolian ancestry. They swoop and dip across the
breadth of his face. Set below heavy black eyebrows, his large
and oval eyes switch from blue to green depending on the
light. Today they are a definite sea-green—swirls of light
around jet-black pupils that bleed into the green like oil on
the ocean.

His nose flares out from under the eyebrows, widening
slightly at the bridge then streaking down to a defined point.
The tip is divided into a subtle cleft, a sublime reference to a
lower, more pronounced beauty.

His mouth is a dark red gash that splits the angular planes of
his face into a rude asymmetrical beauty. His lower lip is fuller
than the upper. It swells out, almost threatening to burst open
like a fig. The upper lip is narrow and lies in elegant submission against the decadence of its companion.

A droplet of ice cream melts and runs down the edge of his
lower lip before dripping onto the floor. A second earlier,
Jerome had licked his finger. The finger he had plunged suddenly into the ice cream and brought up to his chaotic mouth.
As if on cue, there is the screech of brakes as a car pulls up
behind the bus. Jerome's hands tighten imperceptibly around

the handle of the silver scoop. He doesn't need to crane his head out of the glass hatch to see who it is. He steadies himself for a moment against the wooden paneling that lines the interior of the bus. He is fighting his heart that has betrayed him with its sudden acceleration. His penis, which until now has been lying curled against the warmth of his thigh beneath the heavy jeans, thickens. The head, a sleek helmet of velvet flesh, stirs against the rough material.

Jerome stares down at the container of ice cream, at the streaks of raspberry jam swirling through the thick yellow cream like strata of rock. He is reminded of flesh, of the webbing of busy veins carrying life from brain to heart beneath pale skin. There is the slam of a car door, the distant hooting of a horn as another car approaches. In a nearby street a mower starts up.

Jerome looks up at the large clock hanging over the cartons of sugar cones. Two fifteen. He loosens his belt. Another car pulls up on the opposite curb behind the bus. Jerome opens the bar fridge set up on the wall. He plunges his hand into a bucket of ice and delicately pulls out something between his fore- and index fingers that flashes for a moment in the light. It is a large silver ring, too large for a finger, too small for a wrist. He holds it up to his eye. The silver encircles the green. Like this, he has the eye of a bird of prey. Like this, he imagines he can see beyond the bus.

Three steering wheels press against soft breasts. Three mouths twitch in nervous anticipation. Three sets of labia moisten in the still minutes, the moments before movement. Jerome unzips his fly. His cock stands at right angles to his body, its engorged mauve flesh incongruous against the weight of his jeans. Jerome grasps the base with his left hand tightly, close to his balls. With his right he caresses the whole length of it, up over the head, down the shaft. Swiftly, instinctively assessing his own flesh. He bends over the plastic tub of ice cream, scoops up a handful and rubs it slowly over his hot cock. The coolness sends tendrils of pleasure up through his stomach. He rubs the ice cream up and down the shaft, the head bursting a deep scarlet through his sticky fist. With his left hand he slips the ring over the knob down to the base. The cock ring sits nestled against his pubic hair. Now he is ready. Outside three car doors slam shut.

The first woman stands by her green Ford, her eyes flicking from the back of the gray steel bus to the two other women. Her blond hair hangs in a fringe over her eyes, her nervous and thin hands bounce a small red leather purse against her hip. A silence has filled her head.

The second woman catches the first woman's gaze and smiles back—just the merest twitch of the lips in reassurance. Sweating slightly, she pushes back her brown and wavy hair. I own this, she is thinking as she shifts the weight of her well-cushioned hips to the heel of her left shoe. I own this experience. This is my afternoon. She is wet under the armpits and between the legs. She can feel the sun burning the thin skin of her shoulders. She longs to be cool.

The third, a curvaceous Indian, stretches one arm up behind her head, revealing a luxurious bush of jet black underarm hair. She bends down and adjusts her flat leather sandals. The sun hat she's wearing falls off and floats on a hot breeze down along the gutter, to stop at the foot of the huge tire of the bus. Its gentle floating reminds her of a holiday in India she had with her American husband, of him reaching down and catching a wreath of flowers floating down a river. She begins to walk toward the hat.

Her movement is a signal. The brunette first, followed by the blonde. They all move toward the side door of the bus. In the distance an electronic school bell indicating the last lesson goes off.

Jerome pulls the door of the hatch shut. Silently he unlatches the door. He then sits on the counter, his legs spread, his cock rising up from his fly like an aberrant purple popsicle.

The door's rusty hinges squeak in the heat. The Indian woman glides in, confident, the light transforming the shadows on her face into a mottled blue. Then the blonde, smaller and frail-looking. She stands close to the wall, her cheeks the shade of Jerome's deluxe vanilla, paler than cream, warmer than white. Lastly the brunette, who towers over both women, walks noisily into the cabin. The bus rocks slightly with her step. The three standing women make a triangular formation. Not a word is spoken. The Indian woman reaches into the freezer and lifts out a family-sized choc block. Tearing the silver wrapper with her teeth, she peels the foil away from the large chocolate-covered block of ice cream. She places it carefully onto the slab of white marble beside Jerome, taking a sideways glance at the others as she does so. Cold air rises off the ice cream like mist.

Her action is a sign. One woman moves behind her and shrugs off her loose silk shirt. Brown breasts tumble free, sweat glistens between her thin, coffee-colored shoulder blades. In slow synchronicity the three bodies move together. The brunette pulls down the blonde's skirt, slipping it over her hips and letting it fall to the ground. In the same moment the Indian is unfastening the back of the brunette's bra. White breasts bounce into view. Jerome watches silently, quivering slightly in the disturbed air. For one moment the three women are motionless, their skin pale in the filtered light, stockinged legs glittering red and green. Jerome thinks of popsicles in their garish syrups. He thinks of mermaids, of catching fish with his hands, the skin slippery and writhing in the water.

A corner of the ice cream melts away in the heat.

The brunette scoops up a handful of ice cream. Bending forward, she rubs it carefully over Jerome's engorged member. She fastens her lips over the tip and runs her tongue down the shaft. Jerome leans back, a blush spreading up from his neck and across his cheeks, towards those heavy, closed eyelids. Behind the kneeling brunette, the blonde is pressing frozen cherries against the dark flesh of her friend, whose nipples unfurl slowly as the cold red juice runs down to join the droplets of sweat that are beading on her belly. With her head leaning against the steel fridge door, her eyes hooded in pleasure, she gasps as the small blond woman slowly rotates the fruit. Jerome leans down and with his large hands lifts the brunette up over his lap. As she squats, spread and ready, the two other women ease her down onto Jerome's cock.

A trickle of ice cream slips away from the melting choc bloc.

He moves slowly into her. Her sex is completely peeled back, her torso arched, her head, with the wavy brown hair, flung back. The two women move her thighs slowly up and down. Pleasure on a stick. The blonde carefully extends her right hand, her small, thin fingers pull gently at the swollen clitoris. The silence is momentarily broken by a moan. Sweat runs in rivulets between the women's breasts as they move in time. Jerome's cock slips in and out in the center of the room, glistening, the four bodies creating a white-and-chocolate starfish with a blinking red eye in the middle.

I am living in my skin. I think nothing, feel nothing but him entering me, each pore of his velvet skin, thinks the brunette. Each thought is a silver fish, a glint in the heat of sensation. Soon she forgets herself, she has become one huge vulva, her mind has become an enormous sphincter that pulsates with each thrust. She is coming, she is coming.

Her fluttering eyelids are another cue, her moans make her friends move in sympathy, in unison. They want to be taken. The blonde reaches for a popsicle and, falling suddenly to her knees, parts the lips of her impatient friend, flicking the small erect clitoris. With one hand she unpeels the wrapper, nudging the blue tip into the wet mouth of her swollen sex. The Indian grabs a handful of blond hair and presses the blonde's head to her cunt, the salt of sex and the sugary syrup mix. Faster and faster, the blonde thrusts the popsicle in while her warm tongue flicks across the clitoris.

"Sugar and spice and all things nice," the refrain runs through the Indian woman's mind over and over. The image of a huge naked Humpty Dumpty perched on top of a chocolate wall floats before her.

I am going to explode in pleasure, she thinks, *and then melt down into a sugar princess ready to be licked.*

Somewhere in the back of the room the brunette comes in loud cries. The Indian woman wraps her thighs around the blonde, drawing her head right to her sex. Jerome pulls out of the brunette and presses his cock between the buttocks of the kneeling blonde. The Indian watches the two of them, moving like a lissom dancer under water, her movements reflected in the polished steel of the fridge doors as Jerome thrusts in. She can feel the blonde's mouth moving with Jerome's thrusting cock, tongue oscillating. There is nothing but the sound of their panting, of them taking their prompts from each other, quicker and quicker, a measured excitement building. Close to orgasm, the blonde pulls out the popsicle and places it against the anal mouth, drawing up the Indian's thighs so that Jerome can watch, then on cue he too pulls out of the blonde and rests his cock against the smaller, tighter passage. The blonde dips her head and thrusts the popsicle into the Indian's ass, the same time sucking long and hard on her clitoris. Jerome rams into the blonde's ass hole. In one long shout all three orgasm and a hundred ice cream cones, shaken from their box, rain down.

Outside, Quin, driving past in his hired Mustang, notices the old-fashioned silver bus. For a moment he wonders why it shakes and, thinking nothing of it, heads downtown. A seagull perches on the edge of the steel roof. It bends its head to preen under one wing. A sudden movement within the van causes it to lose balance. It flies off in search of puddles.

TULIP

Mischa noticed Deidre long before they met. Cursed with a shyness he masked with aloofness, Mischa had hung back, hiding behind the buckets of irises as he watched his uncle serve her. There was a sadness about her that he empathized with immediately. He recognized the stillness that settled over her like a fine mist once she stopped talking. He knew where her focus went when her eyes got that faraway look.

But where he was lonely, she seemed self-contained. She fitted in with the tall buildings, the constant strobing of light that thrust her into shade and back out into day again, the speed of the pedestrians at lunch hour who rush toward their own separate destinies, oblivious. Would she ever notice him?

Everything about Deidre was immaculate and streamlined, as if she was wary of letting a natural curve break out from under the pressed blouses and suits. There had been enough drama in her younger years, back in the seventies and early eighties. In those days she was married. Dave and Deidre. They were one of those couples that were identified as a unit. They even ran an interior-decorating business together: Dave

would do the design work and Deidre the accounting. Their
marriage was a pleasant haze of work and parties, drunken
cruises on the harbor and Sundays spent smoking pot and
reading the lifestyle pages of the weekend papers in bed.
They became rich together, and increasingly Deidre found
herself not only handling the books, but bringing in the
clients. All was going well.

Until she forgot to take her pill.

In the same week that she discovered she was pregnant,
Dave told her that he'd been having an affair. A day later she
found out that his mistress was in fact a man. After the abortion, an event she refused to grieve over, they separated and
divorced. Deidre, still in shock, had been so reasonable, so
amicable about the whole thing that it was Dave himself who
persuaded her to seek legal representation over the splitting of
their joint assets.

That was 1982. A past client, who had been impressed with
Deidre's chutzpah, offered her a job at the merchant bank he
worked for. Fifteen years later she was still there. It had been a
difficult climb, and although she had finally managed to win
the respect of her employers, the younger men working with
her begrudged her the position she had gained. Rumors of her
sexual frigidity were regularly circulated around the office—
she was known as "the snow duchess" behind her back. Despite
this, Deidre had managed to insulate herself against the
absence of invitations to the marriages, dinner parties and cel-
ebratory lunches over the years, justifying it as a lack of breeding and class on behalf of the voracious young merchant
bankers. Deidre was a snob; it was her anchor in an increasingly bewildering and alienating world.

*   *   *

She reaches the Square. It is a beautiful day, not too hot, with a southerly wind blowing in gently from the harbor. She is heading towards her favorite flower stall, set up near the bronze sculpture of the Tuscany boar, donated to New South Wales by some obscure Italian general. She always visits this flower stall; they have the best selection of flowers, and because she is a regular, Mr. Gretchka gives her a discount. Mr. Gretchka is an elderly Russian, who immigrated here only five years ago. Deidre suspects that he is over-qualified to be running a flower stall. His English is bad but his enthusiasm for Australia and being out of Russia is inspirational.

She stops for a moment in front of the boar. The snout has been polished a shining bronze from the touch of thousands of hopeful hands. It's good luck to make a wish and rub its nose. Interestingly enough the tip of its penis is also a lustrous bronze, rubbed bright by braver people wanting to wish away their loneliness through the hope of some sexual conquest or intimacy. She hesitates. Normally she would touch the end of the snout, but something inside her kicks back, an ennui, a rebellion against all the small routines that make up her life. Before she knows it she finds herself reaching out and touching the end of the boar's penis.

"Double good luck," Mischa ventures. Startled, she whirls around. Standing by the flower stall is a compact young man of Eastern European appearance. He's handsome, but badly dressed in the way of all immigrants from impoverished countries—his seventies jeans finishing unfashionably short on the ankle.

"Fortune favors the brave." He winks at her. For a moment Deidre has to fight off the impulse to look behind her. Then she realizes that the remark is directed at her.

"I'm Mr. Gretchka's nephew. From Russia. You want flowers, yes? He told me about you. You are special customer."

"I want something for my mother, it's her birthday today." As they lean over the flowers, the tentativeness of the young man's gestures undermines his brash selling manner, which she suspects is the product of his uncle's coaching and too many bad American movies.

He suggests Christmas lilies but she thinks they're too funereal. They move on to hyacinths, then a mixed bunch of spring flowers, arguing about the nature of flowers and their psychological properties.

"Daffodils, they are unsubtle, they are the prostitutes of all flowers. They come up from the ground so quickly, with this bright color, standing on the street corner for just a second of the year, and then poof! They're gone! Disappeared. Whores. Much better to buy a flower that is more loyal, that has dignity and will stay around for a lot longer. Like a lily or a tulip that is still closed."

The tone of his voice, his nearness, the vibrancy with which he speaks and his sense of humor ignite something in her body. At first Deidre is terrified that he'll notice. As if she herself has started to exhume a fragrance of her own to attract, like some overblown rose. As he hands her a bunch of lilac, their hands touch just for an instant. A frisson of buried pleasure sparks between them. It is difficult to ignore.

She steps back, internally chastising herself. Don't be ridiculous, you're old enough to be his mother.

"And tonight, are you free?"

"What?"

"Sorry, I am being out of place. A woman such as yourself must surely be busy, yes?"

"Yes."

"Sorry?"

"Yes. Let's go out. I'll meet you at Circular Quay at eight."
There they are, the words. Her heart beats painfully under the
crisp linen suit. This is worse than finalizing a big deal. Get a
grip on yourself.

"Good, at eight then."

She walks off with tulips, dizzy with the new set of deto-
nated chemicals surging through her blood. A date, for the
first time in five years.

Mischa watches her go. She reminds him of the single white
lily, the large blossom always threatening to blow away from
the tall, frail stem. Her pale, serious face perched on that long
neck. Often he'd fantasized about lifting up that fine hair and
kissing her from lip to nipple. He would do it slowly as if collecting the dew of her skin like honey from a flower.

She was turning eighty-two, although officially she'd been in
her late sixties for over a decade. As far as she was concerned
she was the center of the universe and all else should orbit
around her. Deidre was ten minutes late.

"Mauve? Well, I suppose they are rather unusual, although
there is something rather common about tulips."

"Mother, I've given up trying to please you."

"That's evident."

She was impossible to please. Deidre knew that but she fell
into the same emotional trap every time. It must be biological,
a form of genetic envy that makes mothers think that anything
their daughters do isn't good enough.

"How's Wallace?"

"Fine, it took two hours the other night but the prostate
held up."

Wallace was her mother's seventy-eight-year-old boyfriend. They'd met at the casino during one of the pensioners' nights out. Wallace was hopelessly in love with the flirtatious Ethel, who kept him ruthlessly dangling, occasionally allowing him the odd sexual favor.

"You should get yourself a boyfriend. Preferably younger. It's not healthy to be inactive from the neck down."

"I'm not inactive."

"And as for that last slip-up! I knew the moment I saw him, but children never listen. Homosexual. That's why he was so good with the wall papering."

"Interior design, Mother, how many times do I have to tell you? Anyway I've got a boyfriend."

Deidre instantly regretted the words but there they were, sandwiched between the sponge cake and her mother's dentures.

"You have not." Ethel gagged on her cake. For one horrible moment Deidre was terrified that her teeth would go flying. It had happened before.

"Not yet officially, but I am seeing someone, tonight actually."

"He's just after your money." Deidre hated the sinking demoralized feeling her mother provoked in her when she came out with statements like these.

"He might just like me," Deidre put forward, not entirely convinced herself.

"He might. I suppose it's not entirely implausible that he might just find you attractive. Who knows, you might even get laid. Then again, a meteorite could hit Paris."

Matricide had never seemed so attractive as at that moment. Deidre watched her mother's ferocious gesturing as she grumbled about the taxation department. Looking at the pinched skin around her mother's lips, the tightness of her disapproving mouth, as if all the burdens of the world were pressing down on those two thin strips of flesh, reminded her of the aging of her own face. Already she could see echoes of the same lines and the tensions between the eyebrows, around the nose. Eventually Deidre drifted off into a slight reverie, lulled by the scent of the tulips and the talcum powder Ethel used so profusely.

The epic, that's what she craved: to get away from her cantankerous mother; away from her cocoon of stale middle-classdom and decay; away from the bank with its hothouse time that took no account of life cycles.

Her mother burped, discreetly. The clock chimed. Deidre kissed the dry forehead and for an instant regret passed between them like a ghost. Regret for the intimacies they had never made time to share, regret for a history that had made it impossible for them to let their guard down and be friends. Ethel, lost for a moment in the memory of the small child whose hair she used to curl, shook herself back to reality and stroked the hand of this woman, her daughter, who looked so tight and unloved and sad. God bring her joy, the old woman prayed.

Deidre pulled back the door of the cupboard and looked at her naked self long and hard. Harshly, no cheating, just the realities of time staring back at her from the glass. She had a figure like Eve in a van Eyck painting. Unfashionably broad hips that ran into long, thin legs. She extended one and turned her ankle. Her legs were the one thing she really loved about herself. They were good, slim in the thigh, and she frequently wore short skirts to show them off. Still, her skin was firm, she looked good for forty-four years old. She turned sideways and wondered how pregnancy would sit on her frame. She couldn't imagine it. Eight years ago, after the abortion and the divorce, she'd had four unfertilized eggs removed and placed in storage in an IVF clinic. Every year a maintenance invoice for a thousand dollars would arrive in the mail.

Four potential babies.

Deidre didn't really know why she'd done it—a vague hormonal impulse perhaps, somewhere between pragmatism and buried maternal instinct. Always leave your options open was her major premise in life and it had served her well as a banker. Eight years later the eggs were still there, still waiting. She tried to imagine her breasts swollen in their biological destiny. She couldn't.

She picked out a long skirt and a thin silk blouse from the wardrobe. It wasn't too revealing, but she knew she could go without a bra and that her nipples would be just discernible under the silk. Now for the perfume, something light. She hated the heavy, overpowering scents that left you slightly dizzy and nauseous. She chose Chanel No. 19; it was youthful enough to blend in nicely with her own gentle undertones.

Somewhere a phone started ringing. She walked into the bathroom and rescued her mobile from her briefcase.

"Christ, where have you been? I'm having another crisis!" Zoe's dramatic tones bounced off the pale blue tiles and resounded around the large bathroom. Deidre geared herself up. Sometimes she got sick of playing unpaid social worker.

"Let me guess, Justin hasn't rung."

"Not Justin, that was two weeks ago. This one's called Felix and it's a lot worse than that, it's an utter catastrophe!"

"He's run off with your share certificates?"

"He's given me scabies! The whole house is crawling with them."

"Don't you practice safe sex?"

"You don't get it from sex! You get it from normal things like rubbing legs together, sleeping in the same sheets."

"Sounds revolting."

"It's called affection, Deidre, you must have experienced it at least once or twice in your life."

"But I thought you just slept with them for the sex." Zoe broke into a loud wailing. Deidre, used to Zoe's tantrums, would make the obligatory soothing noises at the threats of suicides, face lifts or migration. She had even suggested a couple of psychologists Zoe might try. Today she didn't feel quite so indulgent.

"Well, is it curable?"

"I have to paint my legs with this revolting ointment that stinks of horse piss and wash all the bedding. I'm so upset. I thought he was such a nice man."

"The painter?"

"The video-installation artist. I haven't gone out with a painter for at least a month. This time I thought it was special, we really clicked. There was a real intimacy there."

"You did share diseases."

"God, you're cruel."

"Sorry, I was trying to cheer you up. Guess what I'm doing tonight. I've got a date."

"So you rang that dating service! Good for you, I knew it'd work."

"No, this was spontaneous, you know, destined."

"Destined? Since when have you believed in destiny?"

"I'll tell you about it tomorrow, I don't want to jinx the experience."

"I'll ring tomorrow morning and I expect the phone to be off the hook."

"I don't believe in sex on the first date."

"Darling, if you don't, some other woman will—it's a jungle out there."

"If he wants me, he'll wait. I've got to rush, I'm expected at eight."

"Be bad, and if you can't be bad be worse."

Deidre stared at the phone, suddenly regretting not asking Zoe about how to seduce or at least how to appear seductive. This was what Zoe was best at: she presented herself as a dizzy cloud of blond hair, scent and swaying slim hips that triggered immediate conquistadorial reactions in any man she happened to want that night. What she was bad at was maintaining enough cool, enough emotional objectivity to keep them interested post-orgasm. Dramatic by nature, she immediately sought reassurance that they were committed to her utterly and forever. They naturally left as soon as they could. And she was terribly frightened of growing old alone. This anxiety rose up in that little silence just after sex and overwhelmed Zoe. She needed to be needed, and until Zoe overcame that fear, Deidre philosophized, she would always be alone.

Deidre checked her watch. She had half an hour. Sick with nerves, she tried chanting to herself in the hope that it would relax her. It didn't.

Mischa stands nervously by the Manly ferry terminal. He adjusts his collar. It feels tight, uncomfortable. He is wearing the only suit he possesses, bought on the black market in St.

Petersburg three years ago. Mischa is painfully aware of its broad lapels and baggy trousers. He's only been in Australia for five months and it hasn't been an easy transition. A political history lecturer faced by increasing corruption, he had been forced to give up the country he loved, in spite of its utterly humiliating poverty and a native despair that was neither romantic nor intellectually uplifting.

Here he has found a different kind of poverty—one of experience. Everyone takes everything for granted but complains anyway. For Mischa it is a strange utopia. The bright sunlight that is reflected off the buildings, all new and so modern. The birdsong that at first he'd found so discordant and alien. The endless warmth and indistinguishable seasons which mean you can walk around practically naked all year. The ever-present water, which peeps out at the end of every street, like a shimmering horizon just beyond reach. But for Mischa it lacks sadness, a sense of nostalgia.

He tried to talk about this to his uncle, but he refused to hear anything negative about his beloved city. He attempted to comfort his bewildered nephew by suggesting that it was a lack of history, and that, after a while, the sandstone, the parks, the small terrace houses would organically take on meaning for Mischa, once the young man started to love in this gaudy city. Mischa listened but couldn't imagine this happening—the metropolis was too bright, too elusive in its ever-changing faces.

"Like all Russians, you think too much. For once, just live in your heart. What have you got to lose except worry?" the elder Gretchka had muttered, smiling, pulling on the beard of the younger. He loved this son of his sister. Mischa was the nearest he had to his own flesh and, with poignancy, he recognized many of the dilemmas this tall, vehement 28 year old was going through.

"Get yourself a woman. She will tie you to this city before you have time to put your clothes back on."

His nephew was too serious, and old Mr. Gretchka worried that perhaps the Australian women would be put off by his intensity, his habit of avoiding small talk altogether, his Russian metaphors spoken in broken English with that learnt American accent of his. God knows, he was handsome enough. Like a Russian angel, the old man observed. A shrewd business-man—he'd also observed the number of women who, attracted by the natural grace of his nephew, crossed the square toward the stall. They all left with flowers, but not yet with his nephew's heart.

Mischa rocks on his heels and puts his hand into his pocket. The thought of her has given him an erection. It's then that he sees her walking around the corner. She looks utterly beautiful. He has never seen her out of her work clothes, and the apparition of this tall woman, in her expensive and elegant clothes, makes him pitifully aware of the shameful condition of his own suit. They meet shyly, neither knowing what to do with the moment, but both recognizing the intense attraction between them. He takes her hand like a child's and leads her to the Manly ferry.

From the boat they watch the city transform from a brazen masquerade of advertising and office space into an insect maze of gleaming lights and mirrored windows reflecting the sunset. Overwhelmed by this crystal city, with the blue of the harbor and the foreshore between them, Mischa suddenly loses all his English. This illusion of beauty and wealth was the reason for his migration. The modern splendor of the future, technological and man-made, not like the historical grandeur he'd left behind.

He tries to find the right words but finds himself speaking Russian to this strange woman he's found himself wanting. She replies carefully, having picked up a few Russian words from a colleague.

They stand next to each other, pressed against the rail of the ferry, watching the seagulls riding the air currents and diving down to catch the bread thrown by the passengers. She is acutely aware of the warmth of his body. Taller than her, his hip presses into the hollow of her waist as he vainly tries to shelter her from the wind. They haven't touched deliberately yet, and delicious tremors keep running up Deidre's body. She's been celibate for so long, not just physically but in attitude too, consciously dismissing the possibility of any sexual contact. Now the touch, scent and presence of this vital young man set her hormones into complete revolution. Several times she has to turn away from him.

They find themselves sharing memories and ideas about economies, magic, elderly parents and even the beauty of insects. He doesn't have to hide his eccentricities and quirks, which is his usual way of dealing with women, who are often frightened off by his lateral imagination.

As they talk, every detail of his face, their surroundings, their conversation is intensified to mythic proportions. Deidre feels like she is on drugs or in some weird dream. She sees the city through his eyes as he points out architectural features she'd never noticed before, his long, elegant hands gesturing into the wind. She tries to concentrate on what he is saying, but the beauty of the idiosyncratic details his character has etched into his mannerisms, his slightly crooked smile, the gap between his front teeth, the heaviness of his eyebrows—all distract her. She is thankful when the ferry ride is over and they finally reach the comparative privacy of the restaurant.

He asks her to order for him—Thai food is not something he is familiar with. She asks for honey prawns, crab in green curry and sweet and sour fish balls. She wants to watch him eat. Zoe's comment about how you can tell what kind of lover a man's going to be by the way he eats comes back to her. "Never trust those who are in a hurry to finish; if they don't linger over the entrée, it's wham, bam, thank you ma'am, and one sore pussy—those are the ones who are interested in their orgasm, and not in yours."

Deidre looks across at Mischa; he smiles at her. She looks away. Her vulnerability frightens her. She watches him pick up a prawn and slowly begin to tear off its shell. She hopes he'd be tender and slow; his gestures suggest the touch of a sensualist. She's always found hands the most erotic part of a man. They are like a microcosm of the rest of his body. He's probably got a beautiful penis, she thinks, and blushes. She can't remember the last time she saw or even held one up close. She'd had a disastrous one-night-stand with a sculptor. His proficiency as a lover had intimidated her and she'd spent the whole night apologizing for her clumsiness. She couldn't remember much about that night, certainly nothing as specific as the touch, taste or feel of his cock. She'd consciously dismissed any thoughts about the desirability of men. It was a useful ploy, as she was surrounded by men day in and day out at work. Not that any licentious thought ever passed through her mind while she was there. God forbid! She saw too much of their conniving stratagems. But Mischa was different.

"What are you thinking about?"

"About my work."

"You're a banker, yes?"

"A merchant banker. I help people invest. A lot of the skill is in the timing. But it's all so transient. A deal you've worked on for months comes off and then you're onto the next thing; it's all dependent on the mood of the market place. Sometimes I think I secretly long for something that has a little more permanence."

"You should become a gardener, like me!" He licks the honey off one of the prawns. Deidre can't help notice the sudden pinkness and length of his tongue.

"That way you get to experience real time, plants are good that way. They are dependable. You plant them, you make sure the environment is right, you love, fertilize and water them, then presto! They grow flowers and bear fruit. People and life, this is far more unpredictable. Were you ever married?"

"Once."

"Me too, for about five minutes."

"What happened?"

"She left me for a black marketeer. And you?"

"He left me for our design consultant. We were in business together."

"She must have been ruthless, your design consultant."

"He. And no he wasn't, but they were in love. And sometimes in the face of such a simple truth you have to step aside."

"He left you for another man?"

"It happens. It was a long time ago."

"No children?"

"No. But I did put my eggs on ice. They're frozen, suspended, in case I decide to have them later."

"So it's not too late."

"No, not when you plan ahead."

"Some things you can't plan for, like emotions. To control them would be like trying to control rain or thunder."

He tells her about being involved in the rebellion against Gorbachev and how one of the three martyrs was a personal friend of his. He is passionate about political history. He has a comprehensive overview of Europe, and his understanding of the two world wars and the psychological ramifications of the resulting migration enthral her. She tries out her homespun theories about nationalism and its relationship to territory and economy. He counteracts and challenges her at every point, quoting from Kant, Spinoza, Marx. The titillation of ideas— this is what she finds most sexually stimulating. Collectively their discourse takes shape, sprouting branches and strange fruit. By the end of the meal she feels as if her intellect has been revived with an electricity that has left her feeling alive and capable of anything.

They stand outside her small terrace. Mischa doesn't know whether to touch her or not. He's frightened of overstepping cultural expectations he may be unaware of. He extends his hand. "It has been a beautiful and most stimulating evening."

His sudden formality makes her nervous. She takes his hand and shakes it, wanting him so badly she physically aches, wondering whether she should just pull him toward her and kiss him. It's mathematical, really: the rate of one's fear of rejection is inversely proportionate to the level of desire one feels. The thought etches itself across the recesses of her mind, while her body screams touch him, touch him. If only she had Zoe's confidence.

"Do you . . . ?"

"What?"

"Never mind. I'll see you tomorrow?"

"Of course." With a formal little bow he turns away, and with trembling knees, overwhelmed by a desire to cry, she desperately fumbles with her keys at the front door.

Once inside she bursts into loud sobs, shocking the cat who flees under the couch. She can't believe she could be so foolish, and convinces herself that he didn't find her attractive enough.

Too old, she keeps repeating to herself. Resign yourself to a nun-like existence for the rest of your life. Playing back the picture of him over and over, she throws herself onto the bed and eventually falls into a deep sleep, thankful to feel the effects of the Valium she'd taken swim through her body and pull her down into a dreamless sleep.

Nothing about her appearance the next day indicated any emotional change. She had pulled her hair back into a severe knot, as if to punish herself for the emotional laxity of the night before. She had made up her mind that utter immersion in her work was the only cure for any ridiculous romantic notions she might have indulged in. She was sure that she would never see Mischa again, that his interest in her was merely that of a lonely migrant searching for an intellectual companion, and nothing to do with desire or the potential of a love affair.

The only thing that was difficult to negotiate was a route around the flower stall. This morning she'd walked an extra block to the office and had used the back entrance. The low hum of the computers and the constant sound of the phones and fax machines obliterated the possibility of debating internally on what could have been a great love affair, or at least one night of bliss. She adjusted the silk scarf around her neck and walked briskly up to her desk. Already there were four faxes from Tokyo and a couple of messages from her various clients.

She booted up her screen and checked out the overnight figures for the Nikkei. An inner voice kept saying gold, gold. Several snippets of information were being pieced together in her brain. Other bankers credited her with intuition, a natural hunch about what to buy and when to sell, but there was nothing magical or mysterious about Deidre's ability to second-guess the marketplace. It was the fastidious collection of information and the knack of fitting it all together in a lateral jigsaw that made her an exceptional banker. Why she hadn't been promoted was something her colleagues didn't like to speculate on, knowing that it was only her gender that kept her out of the inner sanctum. She was on a hundred and fifty thousand a year, but what she made the bank was over fifty times that amount.

She looked up gold. Stocks were down on all the major markets, but the idea kept gnawing at her. There was a remark she'd overheard, that article about new mining technology in *New Scientist*, a fall in the Hang Seng, a mine in Western Australia that had been using the techniques for a least a year. Finally, that Gutnick tip she'd had from one of her clients. Coles-Myer needed to invest a hundred thousand, she could start with them. If she bought now while the prices were low she could come out on top, perhaps sooner than people suspected.

Fifteen minutes later she was standing in the office of Edward Short, her immediate superior and CEO of the investment branch of the bank. A balding man in his late fifties,

Edward had recently left his wife of twenty-five years to marry his secretary, fifteen years his junior. He hated Deidre. He found her manner inherently arrogant, but the fact that she never bothered to socialize with the other bankers also made it difficult for him to muster up enthusiasm for her. Sometimes he was convinced that she was passing some covert moral judgment on his behavior. She also strongly reminded him of his mother. But in the past ten years she had introduced fifteen major clients to the bank, and her investment record was such that the clients refused to deal with anyone else.

Deidre assumed that Edward was awkward with her because he was uncomfortable with all intellectual equals, especially if they were female. She trusted him nevertheless.

"Gold. There's this small mine, east of Coolgardie. McHuen's. I want to buy."

"Gold is down at the moment."

"I have a strong feeling—you know, one of my blindingly insightful flashes."

"Leave it with me, don't buy just yet, give it a day or two."

"It's going to go now, I know it."

"Hey, trust me on this."

"Fortune favors the brave."

"Wait a week."

She grimaced but reluctantly assented. "OK, but then I'm buying."

He spun around in his chair as soon as she'd left the room, waving and pulling a funny face at her back as he watched her walk out of earshot down the corridor. As soon as she disappeared he picked up his phone.

"Harry? Pick me up twenty thou on gold. A small company called McHuen's. No questions, OK?"

*   *   *

Deidre walks back into the dealers' area. One broker, a young gun in his early twenties, is busy shaving while negotiating a deal on the phone. He's only been with the company for eight months, yet he's already on the same salary as Deidre. She checks the trade index figures.

"Congratulations on the Fuji deal. Only you could have pulled that one off."

"Yeah, nerves of steel." He turns and in an undertone mutters to his mate, "And heart of ice." She catches the words faintly, but ignores them.

"Deidre!"

A ripple runs through the banking floor, new blood has entered the arena—she can practically see the testosterone bristling. She turns. Mischa, dressed in his suit and clutching a huge bunch of roses, stands in the center of the floor. He smiles at her. Everyone swings around and stares surprised as Deidre walks up to him.

"I brought you these. I think maybe I insulted you last night." Deidre, acutely aware of the grinning faces, leads Mischa toward the door.

"This isn't the place to talk."

"Are you ashamed that you know me?"

"It isn't that. The people here, the men, they think I'm a snow duchess."

"Snow duchess? Is this a good thing?"

"It means that I'm frigid. Cold like snow."

"They are fools."

Several of the bankers snigger.

"Mr. Gretchka, I think we should discuss your portfolio in my office."

She formally walks him out into the corridor. Outside he grabs her hand and leads her toward the fire escape.

"Where does this lead?"

"To the roof."

Holding her hand he starts climbing. She follows, half of her fighting to regain control, the other half drawn by the determination of this young man. He pushes the trapdoor open, revealing a small square of blue.

Once outside, the view is spectacular, revealing the whole panorama of the city of Sydney. Church spirals butted up against the skyscrapers set in stark relief against the horizon. To the north looms the Bridge, the Opera House nestling like a jewel in a belly button, at its base. Beyond them the harbor shimmers, tantalizing in the summer heat.

"It's beautiful, like heaven," he whispers as if he is in church. She smiles and traces a bead of sweat running from his cheek to his lips. As her fingers caress the soft young skin he catches her between his lips, drawing her into his mouth with his teeth and pulling her toward him. He wraps his legs around her. Her heartbeat quickens as she feels the shape of his erection pressing into her skirt. This moment of discovery never fails to astound her.

They roll gently down the slope of the roof. He holds on to her as they turn slowly, the spinning azure sky blending with the red of his shirt, the soft gray of the roof as they turn over and over, arriving at the shallow base of the roofline. He takes his jacket off and spreads it on the tarmac surface. The heat rises up and she can smell the hot tar mixed in with the scent of flowers floating up from the botanical gardens.

He is kneeling—waiting for her. She stands by him, bending slightly in the warm wind, her eyes closed. Without thought. Just the music of the city and the anticipation of his touch. She feels his hands running up her legs, up to her center. With her eyes still closed, she focuses on this sensation, the roar of the cars below and the sound of a plane passing overhead all melting into the tips of his fingers. He strokes the softest part of her skin, the inside of her thighs, drawing tiny circles with his finger tips. She can hardly stand for the sheer pleasure. Slowly he runs his fingers around the edge of her pants, caressing her outer lips and pulling them back a little so that her clitoris is pushed hard against the cloth. She wants him to slip one, two, three fingers into her. She wants his cock. Without saying a word he pushes her tights and pants down to her ankles.

"Please, just stand there for a moment." She stands exposed, the wind blowing up her skirt, on top of the world, on top of this blind city. To be naked and so close to the thousands of workers hidden behind a multitude of mirrored windows. Prisms of intrigue. A thousand afternoons. A thousand moments like these.

She wonders if they are being watched. She hopes so. The idea empowers her, the danger of it excites her. He lifts her skirt up over her head and helps her out of the rest of her clothes. She is now completely naked.

He takes a rose and traces it across her face, trailing the heavy perfume over her nose and lips, the petals catching the surface of her skin and sending a tingling right down to her groin. He kneels in front of her and runs the rose down the whole length of her body, crushing the juice of the petals as he does so, anointing her with the scent. The aroma, pungent and sweet, rises and overwhelms her for a second. He peels her open, revealing the mouth of her sex, her clit, which stands erect like a tiny stamen. He touches her, running his fingers across and around, over and over. She quivers, wanting the man, wanting the cock. She sinks to her knees and frantically struggles to free him. He springs, long and erect. She lowers her head and takes him into her mouth. She wants all of him, now.

He pulls away from her and lowers her gently onto his jacket. She lies there pinned, waiting, wanting. He grabs a handful of the roses and showers the petals onto her. They float down falling across her breasts and belly. Watching her face he plays with her, making her gasp with each new caress. Leaning over her, teasing her with his cock, he weaves a path with the tip through the layers of rose petals which fall across her hair, her eyes. She wants him so badly, she's burning, but still he holds her down, strumming her clit softly, excruciating pleasure. Unable to contain herself she pulls him toward her, kissing him deeply, taking his tongue deeply into her mouth. The rose petals crushed become a slippery layer between them. Her urgency inflames his own as she guides him. Diving into her, skin on skin, the consummation, the ecstasy of him in her, filling her, releasing her. His lips are everywhere, kissing and licking her breasts, biting her ears, her neck. She is lost in her own passion, wanting to take him, to be in control. She throws him over onto his back and rides him, the length of him making her gasp. Disturbed, a flock of pigeons scatter up into the warm air currents, cooing in approval. He quickens his tempo in response to hers until she is unable to discern where her flesh ends and his begins. A ball of pleasure rolls up from the base of her womb and like an avalanche rips through her body. A moment later, triggered by her frenzy, he comes too, his whole body involuntarily jolting as his seed bolts through her.

*   *   *

"Pretty adventurous for a senior executive," Edward's voice booms across the roof. Deidre lifts herself up onto her elbows and scrambles to cover herself. "But not acceptable to company policy. I'll see you in my office."

Edward squints in the sun, trying unsuccessfully to retain his dignity as he stumbles across the roof before disappearing onto the fire escape.

"Who was that?"

"My boss. How long do you think he'd been standing there?"

"I don't know. I was a little distracted." He kisses her mouth and her damp nipples. She lets herself be lulled for a moment, but, remembering the look on Edward's face, she stands up and starts pulling on her clothes.

"Go down the fire exit, it will take you directly out onto the street."

"When do I see you?"

"I don't know."

"Tonight. I will be at your house at nine, okay?" He doesn't wait for her answer, and kisses her before disappearing through the trapdoor. She slips on her shoes and dusts the back of her skirt. A sudden silence engulfs her as a startled pigeon flaps chaotically up toward the sky. Nothing will be the same, she knows that now. Her world, the constructs she has so carefully built around herself, are now rendered irrelevant. Inside the cool, shadowy stairwell she leans against the wall and starts to laugh.

Later that day Edward fired her, claiming that her behavior was untenable and too morally undermining for the company to sustain. Deidre suffered his hypocrisy silently. It was a well-publicized fact that he'd had regular liaisons with his secretary on the very same roof.

Many found it inconceivable that Deidre would suddenly break out sexually like that. Muttering quietly amongst themselves, they put it down to stress or menopause. But, as the weeks passed, her absence grew like a tumor.

Two weeks later Mischa arrived at her house carrying three cheap suitcases and four cartons of old Russian paperbacks. Deidre was amazed at the ease with which she gave up her territory: his guitar was propped up against her desk, his few toiletries balanced against her own on top of the bathroom cabinet, his old leather coat made an unnoticed entry beside her own linen jacket. Even holding his shaving brush gave her a secret thrill.

Time took on its natural cycles. Just before dawn she would wake and watch as Mischa slept, his long lashes curled over his cheeks, the vulnerability of his hands and arms as she lay spooned around him, her hands wrapped around his soft cock.

Three generations of his life shifted and flitted across his face. Child, boy, young man.

She couldn't believe that he was still in her bed, that this could happen to her so easily after all these years. She kept thinking that at any minute a disaster would occur that would destroy her rapture. If he was late she would sit by the phone terrified that he'd been killed in a car accident or detained under some immigration law he'd contravened without telling her.

Zoe was initially incredulous that Deidre had not only managed to find a boyfriend but had then kept the relationship going. As days became weeks, the initial awe turned to envy.

She kept finding fault with Mischa: he's too young, too foreign, not ambitious enough . . . the litany went on. As for Mischa, he found Zoe's attempts at flirtation distasteful and disloyal. But, ever discreet, he maintained a diplomatic silence.

Mischa also understood the importance of seducing the mother as well as the daughter. Ethel found the young man cosmopolitan and dedicated to Deidre, and being an amateur gardener herself would try Mischa's patience by engaging him in long soliloquies about the correct way to grow magnolias, or how to get rid of black spot on roses. She didn't care about the age difference between them, herself being of that age where time gives you the benefit of wisdom and tolerance.

"Happiness is so transitory, dear," she told Deidre. "When you have it, grab it with both hands and hold on tightly."

Deidre would spend hours in the small walled garden that Mischa had now planted with exotic purple and magenta blossoms. Under his guidance she read the contemporary philosophers and began to explore some of the more recent theories of physics and spirituality.

Sitting there in the shade, the roar of the traffic a distant hum, she'd fall into a reverie watching a caterpillar climbing painstakingly up the stem of a plant. She felt as if the vegetation around her was ripening, swelling in preparation for something. A seed had been sown, but what fruit it was to bear she abandoned to destiny.

She lowers herself carefully onto the hospital trolley, already her flesh feels precious. Mischa, walking beside her, slips a small Russian doll into her hand. She opens it up, inside is a tiny pearl.

"This will be you."

"It might not work." She can't keep the anxiety out of her voice.

"Maybe not now, but I know it will eventually. I love you."

Smiling, he disappears for a second as they enter the clinic through separate doors. As the attendants slip her onto the bed, Mischa reappears in a green hospital gown and picks up a stethoscope lying on the small operating table beside the bed. He puts the ear pieces into her ears and places the end over his heart.

"You see? My heart runs with yours . . ."

She laughs, the accidental poetry of his grammar still making her melt.

"Hearts don't run, they race."

"Race? We are lovers not athletes."

"Mischa, I'm scared."

He kisses her.

"Don't be."

The nurse starts to pull the screens around and Deidre reaches for Mischa's hand. Her heart is, indeed, running. She gazes up at the ceiling with its fluorescent light, blinking slightly.

Mischa squeezes her hand. "You OK?" he whispers.

She smiles up at him. Any minute now the surgeon will inject the fertilized eggs into her womb.

"I'm trying to visualize what she'll look like."

"It could be a boy."

"It could."

Mischa leans down and kisses her. Suddenly she wants to cry.

THE LISTENING ROOM

I have always found the concept of hell vaguely exciting, a sort of pornographic Bosch scenario, devils with weasel heads and huge phalluses impaling pale golden maidens, buttocks parted, hands bound ruthlessly behind . . .

Looking up from her book, she crosses her legs. She feels herself becoming moist. Outside the bus, the lights of the city sail past. It's a summer night, the kind of heat that excites, making everything seem possible.

She is still young. She sits there, book in lap, feeling the perimeters of her body under the tight satin dress, the underwire of her bra pushing up her breasts. Sweat runs between the tight material and her waist. She shifts her weight, peeling one buttock from the plastic seat. Everything vibrating under her skin. She looks back down at the book, a deconstruction of sexuality, a birthday present from him.

As I play back the images I become both the taken and the taker.

PORN TALK: HER

He pushes me against the door, his hard cock pressing against me through his trousers. He pulls up my skirt, thrusting his hand down my underpants and finding the tip of my clit. Gently, he teases it until it is big enough to pull at between his fingers. I fall moaning against the wall.

PORN TALK: HIM

She runs her tongue along the underside of my cock. I push back her lips with my fingers; her mouth is soft, sucking. She takes me into her, sucking deeply, her tongue a ring of fire. I'm gonna explode, her hot wet pussy lies spread on the pillow. I find her clit. As I suck, it grows like a little cock. She thrashes about, losing control as I ram deeper and deeper into her throat.

As she reads she is being watched. She glances up; two men are sitting opposite her. Their eyes have hope. The briefcase at her feet falls to the floor as the bus lurches around the corner. Quickly she rights it. If only they knew, the people on the bus, if only they knew what was inside.

There is a schism in me, between the erotic and the intimate. One, by definition, negates the other. For me the pursuit of sensuality for its own sake without the confines of emotional expectation or history is a freeing of the libido, standing outside of marriage, conception, emotional obligation. The subject becomes object. Object is the ascetic, the visual moment, no past, no future, just the moment of orgasm. This is not exclusively male territory. The encounter is, by its very nature, transitory.

She relates to these words, her own domesticity crushing down on her. A chosen oppression. A misguided impulse to appear as others. Impossible. Truth, like Nature, always finds a way through the cement.

Last night I dreamt about a gorilla, a large, sad primate. He was standing in the middle of the lounge room. His bulk was impressive and he knew it. Over seven foot in height with shaggy fur that hung down to the carpet. He had been chasing me all around the house. My family, that is my mother, brother and sister, who is always eight years old in my dreams, hid behind the couch terrified. His cage sat on the lawn outside the house. The cage door swung open in the breeze. He stood in the middle of the lounge room, opened his arms and began to reason with me in a deep melodious voice.

"What harm can I do you, little girl? All I want to do to you is hug you, wrap you up in my long smelly arms. Come here, just a little further, just a little further . . ." I walked bravely to the center of the room and began to argue sexual politics with him.

On the other side of Westminster Bridge stands the arts center, a fortress of concrete and glass, and the old river reflecting back this stark oasis. Next to it is the concert hall. Inside, a large body of people sit in the auditorium, waiting for the conductor to raise his baton. The conductor is her husband. He is fifty-two years old. Four back teeth in the lower jaw are false. He has a scar below his right nipple where he fell into a rose bush as a young boy. His penis is thick and slightly bent to the left. He is uncircumcised. At the moment he is slightly tumescent. This is because he is about to perform. The vibrations of the music play against the pleasure lobes at the back of his neck and he grows hard. But not too hard. Tumescent or not, the young woman loves her husband, all of him, and his four back teeth, but mostly she loves his smell.

The bus stops.

A young man comes aboard: I can see only his shoulders at first. Broad shoulders, shoulders you don't roll off. He leans against the glass partition with his back to me. He wears a dark scarlet silk shirt, I can see the texture pushed up against the glass. Just as I can see the tapering waist, the slim hips, the outline of his buttocks pressed against the glass. The conductor sits at the other end absorbed in a comic. Apart from him we are the only people on the bus. His hands hang down by his sides, tanned hands, with long, tapering fingers. He feels in his pockets with his left hand and pulls out a key ring, a silver orb. He rolls this from one finger to another. Swiftly, deftly.

I wonder if he is a magician.

She wonders about his cock, the shape of it, the weight of it, the taste of it. The bulk of his body promises size. He hasn't turned around, but he wears his body comfortably, with the confidence of attractive people. His hair is thick, Celtic-black. It falls just below the collar of his shirt. For a moment she tastes salt in her mouth.

The man in the bus turns. His face comes into profile. With the alertness of those who are watched, he moves across and sits opposite her. She drops her eyes immediately as his gaze burns across her cheek, her breasts, her shifting legs. He sees the face of a woman, an innocence masking a terrible curiosity. A strong chin; olive skin with a faint moustache that highlights the edge of the upper lip. A fuller lower lip, her eyebrows feline. Black semicircles in a pale circle. The eyelids protrude knowingly. It is her eyes he wants to fuck. She sees the black down on the fingers of his hands. The long black hair escaping from his shirt sleeves. The jawline sweeping up from the pronounced bones in the neck. His white skin. The scarred pores that push the aquiline into animal. The blind flesh in the trousers. His tongue for a second. And the gray of his eyes that shutters like the flash gun of a camera when their eyes meet.

The woman knows. The woman knows she has a choice. She could stand up and press the button and descend from the bus. Or she could stay sitting there opposite him, pinned into the sticky seat. The air congealing between them until it threatens to fall from the ceiling in thick white strings of risk, of fear, of expectation. Or she could lean across and, kneeling, open his flesh to her hand. Her hot cunt. Her empty mouth. I am now, not then or tomorrow. But now. And I will take what I want now and this gesture will stay crystallized. Inevitable, fatal, standing outside of time.

The moment threatens to pass stretching thin, the smell of his sweat and aftershave under the tobacco sweeping across as the bus door opens. She feels dizzy. Her pupils dilate and her lips swell. Beneath her skirt her cunt grows wet as if he has touched her. Their eyes are talking, they are saying, Let me peel back your skin, and I will make you scream, tear you a little. I will hold your legs between my thick thighs and squeeze until it is bone on bone, flesh on flesh and we are animal again. Promise. I want to drink you inside, swallow you whole so that your flesh fills me right through to the hip bone. I want you to fill every orifice. Get inside me, under my skin, under my pumping heart.

Silence talks. She stands and turns. The seam of her fishnet tights halves her vulva, secretly sticky. She reaches up, conscious of the circumference of her body, stretching just a little bit further to let him know. As if he needs telling.

Behind her she feels the air shift as he stands. She dare not run for fear he will use sound, break the smell that tugs, the blind clenching of cock and cunt. Please, she prays, stay without history, without pathos, without darling darling do you love me, so that I can think again with my skin. The man stays silent. He stands and presses the button for the next stop.

They both step off the bus, his footsteps echoing behind her, slightly to her left. In her heart there are four empty chambers and two sets of heart strings. Fear dries her mouth. She is listening for trust in his step so that the pictures in her head fit with the hiss of the summer rain hitting the pavement. He is right behind her. He is with her all the way. They walk toward the concert hall.

Inside, her husband lifts his baton and the harpist runs her long fingers down three octaves.

Around them, invisible spirits swirl and seep into the cortex but these two pause for a second. They are standing outside the large windows of the concert hall. Inside is all gilt and warm red leather. Music is audible. It floats out in cold streams like the air-conditioning.

She steps inside and he follows, shadowing her along the leather-lined corridors. Her hand trails for a moment across the padded stretched skin. It makes her think of large square cows, and how much grass they'd have to eat to cover a concert hall. Under her hand she thinks she can feel the audience breathing through the leather. There are attendants standing at the entry of the foyer selling programs. Her husband, hair dyed, twenty years younger, smiles from the cover. He is a vain man. A successful, handsome man.

The program booth is situated under a strange painting. It catches her eye. Semiabstract, with great swirling arcs of red, it seems to represent two women making love. Their pose reminds her of early Chinese erotica. It has the same naive joy. She stops and buys a program, and the young attendant smiles at her as she hands her the change.

"The concert's already started, Mrs. Pope, but I'm sure you'd be able to watch from the listening room." She smiles again. The woman wonders if the attendant has slept with her husband. The young man stands facing a framed photo, an image of Mr. Pope, his eyes bright and slightly salacious, hair elegantly ruffled in a thin attempt to look casual, the gap between nose and upper lip betraying a Romanian heritage.

She watches him look at the photo of her husband. He gazes up at the image, his weight poised forward. He turns and smiles at her and carefully raises his hand in exactly the same gesture, in a parody without malice.

She is amused and suddenly she is older, in control. She takes his hand and leads him down the corridor.

She has this image in her head from when she grew up. When she traveled on the subway with her grandmother she would stare at the large colorful posters pasted on the opposite walls of the platform. There was one particular poster: an advertisement for Clarks shoes with two little children, Hansel and Gretel, walking down a path leading into a huge dark green forest.

She would stand on the edge of the train platform and look into the poster. It seemed as if the path stretched into a sinister, leafy infinity. The thought that the two children would walk together in this manner with no destiny in sight induced a breathlessness in her, a suffocation. It was this disembodiment she felt now, as if she was looking down at herself and this unfamiliar young man. The deliberation involved in being the leader, acting upon one's fantasies. A decision has been made.

They reach a small red door set into the wall of the auditorium. The music playing within is audible and vibrates beneath their feet. The brass section reaches a crescendo and she can see the exact stance of her husband, both hands jerking up in that curious half-knowing, half-abandoned impulse which music, like electricity, induces in him. His face will be wildly out of control, revealing a sensuality he has never been able to express. The trumpets stop and the string section begins a low wailing. When she first saw him like this she knew that she loved him.

Mr. and Mrs. Pope have been married for eighteen months. He is the only man she knows who does not ultimately bore her, and in the moments that her interest lapses all she has to do is watch him raise his baton. She is the only woman he knows who can spontaneously orgasm to Mahler. Her favorite is the *Resurrection*.

She reaches into her briefcase and pulls out a small gold key. She unlocks the door.

Gently he pushes her in from behind, and she stumbles into the darkened room. The sound of the music is near-deafening. He places his hands over her breasts, caressing the orbs, pulling at the nipples. They harden beneath the satin. She pushes the door shut with her foot.

The room is small, set into the left wall of the auditorium facing the stage. Ordinarily it is used for the recording of concerts by the BBC. The proximity of the stage and the acoustics incurred by such geography make this possible. It is twelve feet long and four feet wide with wood paneling. Two large windows open directly onto the auditorium and face the stage.

The room is about twenty feet away from the front of the stage, thus enabling a complete panoramic view of both conductor and orchestra. Because of its darkened walls and the manner in which the windows are set slightly above and into the walls of the auditorium, both audience and performers are oblivious to the existence of the room unless otherwise informed.

It was Mr. Pope who initially encouraged his wife to use it as a kind of private listening room. At this very moment he is thinking about her sitting alone, her head tilted to one side, watching him. The thought of her watching him increases his tumescence. He is a performer by nature, some might say it was imprinted on his DNA. He only becomes sexually excited when he knows he is being watched. Too many easy conquests have left him jaded and satiated, an affliction that has intensified with middle age. Each new seduction is the only way he can reach out, touch the persona they are selling to the public. Not his private self, he left that on a train fleeing Romania somewhere in the mid-fifties. To know himself he needs to be told about himself, preferably from the lips of young girls. Otherwise after each concert tour his sense of identity spirals down into a void without meaning.

Mr. Pope raises his baton and the cellist begins the second movement. Mrs. Pope pushes the young man away from her. She gestures for him to keep quiet. Slowly, from within her briefcase, she pulls out a black net corset and two highly polished Italian patent-leather pumps. She bends over, and the man begins rolling her skirt above her hips. She stands and pushes her skirt back down. He moves across the darkened room and leans into the window. Just then the conductor raises his arms and with a wild flailing sweeps the orchestra into the second movement. She slips on the corset under her dress, a quarter-cup black number. The cups cut under her breasts, as if a man is holding them up and squeezing them.

She begins rolling down her fishnet tights. They catch slightly on her toenails. She turns to the young man.

His head is nodding in time with the music. He leans against the wide shelf of the window, beyond which she can see her husband vacillate with the music. At that instance she can see through the young man's eyes. She knows what stirs him beneath his trousers. It is the proximity of the audience just outside the window. The smell of the collective animal, the French perfume, the sweat, the secret undersmells that whisper. It fills the room. They are her captive audience, blind to her presence yet so close that if she wanted to she could throw her lingerie and it would fall, perhaps dangle, across their faces.

On stage, the fourth violinist studies a twist of blond hair. It curls teasingly on the neck of the cellist sitting in front of him. The fourth violinist, barely nineteen and still a virgin, wonders what the hair would taste like. He imagines salty. He imagines running his fingers up the smooth nape then plunging his fingers into the soft mass of hair. Taking a handful he would push her head down, push her soft pliant mouth down to his cock and . . . the third violinist nudges him hard in the ribs. He is late with his note by twenty seconds.

He follows the conductor's baton as it spirals slowly up into the air. His eye is caught by something set into the wall.

WHAT THE FOURTH VIOLINIST SEES

He sees the pale face of a beautiful man, not much older than himself, who sits watching in the window of the listening room. There is something odd about the slightly disjointed way the beautiful man nods his head to the music.

Two white breasts seem to float toward the young man. A woman, older, her hair loose, torso poured into a corset, pushes her breasts towards his face. He takes one fully into his mouth. The fourth violinist sees the long nipple disappearing into the young man's full lips. In and out. In and out. Again the fourth violinist misses his cue.

WHAT MRS. POPE FEELS

Teeth around the nipple teasing slightly, biting, circling with his tongue as the nipple hardens, then slowly sucking. Quicker, quicker. He takes the other breast, pulling harder, rolling the nipple between his two fingers. He plays my body, he plays my breasts. He is a sex child. I am a mother with a cunt. Red threads run from my nipple to my navel, a lattice of pleasure. I want him to touch my sex. I move forward but he holds me at a distance. He knows what he's doing and he's in no hurry.

WHAT THE SILENT YOUNG MAN FEELS

Skin. Skin you can press your fingers into, sinking, sinking. Skin like sweet warm milk. The blue veins run like water just below the surface. Breasts that run in a perfect semi-circle below the nipple, large, unmistakable. Her raised areola tastes like plums. Bruised plums with a slight tang of sea salt. I want her to take me like a young siren, Medusa lashed to the deck. And all around the churning sea.

WHAT THE HUSBAND IS THINKING

Why do you want to know? It doesn't matter what I think. I am just a bit player, a construct of Katherine's. That's her name, Katherine Pope née Handsworth. I stand here and I am not entirely conscious. Musical instinct drives me. I hear the notes before they are played. I am orchestrating the moment before it manifests. This makes me the dictator. The puppet master with a hundred invisible strings attached to the lips and instruments of the orchestra in front of me. This power is tremendously exciting. The responsibility involved is also terrifying. I can feel the audience breathing at the back of my neck. They inhale as one. Their breath travels in languid rivulets that accelerate with the music. As the master I feel as if I am choreographing one enormous collective orgasm . . . or perhaps a series of little climaxes that lead to a kind of death. The kind of death that sears the top of the brain as the whole orchestra concludes in a concoction of violent color, leaving you floating somewhere near the chandeliers.

The kind of death that occurs in the silence between the last note and rapturous applause. The last heartbeat.

Notation: Climax. Beat. Silence. Beat. Applause.

I like to think I specifically cater for the women in the audience. For the older blue-rinse set, the gentler, slower ascent is kinder on bodies familiar with touch.

For the younger frisky members (and God knows the numbers are dwindling) I direct the triumphant heroics of the brass section. For the men I leave the space between the notes, they can draw their own conclusions.

You tell me my wife is in the audience. I know that already, I feel it. There is a symbiosis between even warring couples. *Comprenez-vous?* Not that I don't love my wife. It's just that she is so different. For her life is still dramatic. The pathos she generates throws everything up into a sharper focus. That's why I love her, she wakes me up. And there's only two things that wake me up. Fellatio and Mozart.

WHAT THE FOURTH VIOLINIST SEES

He lifts her up and pulls her onto his lap. The fourth violinist falters for a moment as the woman clutches at the man's cock. Even in the shadows he can see the length and thickness clearly, a thick conquering phallus that makes a frail silhouette of the rest of the body. The man's profile is Bacchus, Priapus, Jack of the Beanstalk. She drops to her knees. Her breasts pour over his glans, he plunges into the cleavage.

The fourth violinist's bow drops to the floor, the bassist covers for him. As he reaches down he notices the slim ankles of the cellist. He imagines soft ridges of blond hair running inside thighs to a golden bush. As he sits there he glances across to the listening room again. The woman is taking the man into her mouth.

The fourth violinist imagines the feel of her mouth, the way her tongue would play under the ridge like a wind instrument. He wonders about the flautist.

The woman's head bobs up and down as she takes all of it deep into her throat, the man flings back his head, his mouth open in ecstacy. As they reach the conclusion of the third movement he pulls her away, holding himself tightly at the base of his shaft, saving himself. The fourth violinist glances at the third violinist, instrument poised in mid-air, his face flushed. He too stares in the direction of the listening room.

WHAT MRS. POPE FEELS

The taste of him is youth, slightly pungent, the aroma of almonds and hot testicles. Velvet, heavy in the palm, pushing against my belly. The blind beast that splits the peach. What could I do? I dropped to my knees and tasted him.

He seeps a droplet of the ocean, and I suck. I swallow him. Feeling him quivering under the tongue, this makes me master. As I suck I see my husband, racing with the music. Waves of red and white spirals interlace with the music and press against my eyes.

He pushes against the back of my throat, his urgency becomes mine. Faster, faster, I press my clit against the back of my heel, rubbing against the soft Italian leather. Faster, faster, louder, the music, the salt, the chorus of male voices, the pulse of his seed, of my wet sex. He pulls away and turns me around. Parting my buttocks, he plunges in, drawing me down onto his lap. Into the sphere of his chest, his smell. Tongue in my ear, one hand holding me apart, the other squeezing my breasts, as if he is trying to feel all flesh at once. And I am big. I am bursting with juice. And he plunges and rises, guiding me over the tip, then slowly down onto the shaft. Fast, faster, faster still. All is wet. The walls of Jericho have tumbled down.

WHAT THE SILENT YOUNG MAN FEELS

All I know is her flesh, the tone of her voice and her scent, her fingers wiser than mine. They don't hesitate. Her cunt is a tight veil. I draw it across my face, my lips, over the skin of my body until she is welded to my belly. I want to fill every hole, her ass, her cunt, her ear, her mouth. To fuck you and the strangeness inside you. Her breasts fill my hands, they are flesh at the end of a tight wet canal. We are riding the waves, and the ceiling drips song.

When I fuck you I am fucking your husband. I shut my eyes and it is his hands grasping the baton. The jerking stick, my cock, your music. Your moaning under our breath. This is what I feel.

WHAT THE HUSBAND IS THINKING

Something's missing in the string section. Come in, come in, you bastards. The third and fourth. They're not even looking at their scores. I'll tap the music stand. What are they staring at? Ahh at last, a note. Thank you gentlemen . . . slowly, slowly, gently, gently, think about a tiny silver sea lapping between your toes, drawing up over the ankles, not too fast . . . washing up like waves of electricity over the knees.

HER

He's lifting me up onto the broad windowsill, the hot air of the auditorium warms my buttocks. He parts my lips and buries his mouth, finding my clit, playing me with his tongue. I moan. My body trembles under his fingers. Just the tip, just the tip, then as I grow he takes all of me and sucks . . . It is as if he is inside all of me, as if my pleasure is his.

THE SILENT YOUNG MAN

The smell of her, the taste of her . . . the flesh quivers, a tiny penis, she is close to coming. I am pulling her to her feet, I'm wrapping her legs around my hips. I press her against the wall and cut into her like a hot knife through butter.

THE HUSBAND

Up over the waist, bring in drums, that's it! That's it! Nail the rhythm into the guts, into the very core of being! Faster! Faster! Faster! And cut! Now the death, now the silence rushing in.

HER

Ahhhhhh!

THE SILENT YOUNG MAN

Ahhhhhh!

THE HUSBAND

Screams pierce the silence between crescendo and applause. I swing around, furious. A couple lie satiated, half naked, hanging out of the window of the listening room.

It is an image from my worst nightmare. It is not real. Her long red hair cascading down the wall. The older members of the orchestra start to cough, to avert their eyes. The younger members grin openly. It is a phantasm. The young man pulls himself out of my wife and smiles slowly. He takes a bow.

The whole auditorium is shaking with laughter.

There is no applause.

LOOKING FOR STRANGE

THE LOVER

All that is visible is the radio alarm clock sitting on a table by the side of the bed. Its faint glow also illuminates the bed's white quilted spread, which I have drawn up as far as my nose. It smells of her. And me. I lie there, feeling the tension ooze out of my feet, the muscles at the back of my neck, my stomach. We finished making love only ten minutes ago. But I like to lie here, alone in her flat after she's gone to work. It gives me time to explore.

I swing my legs out of the bed. A thick rug of some foreign material lies in the middle of cool polished floorboards. When I sink my toes into it, the carpet releases an exotic fragrance. She once told me that nomads used to play chess on it. And here it is, marooned in a Tasmanian suburb.

There is a dresser against the wall, a heavy antique piece with brass claws for feet, clutching, alive. The dresser is strewn with tiny pots of cosmetics, necklaces glittering dimly in the dark, an abandoned velvet sash, a hairbrush that smells of old hair spray, perfume and the darker scent of olive skin and thick black hair. I hover for a moment, but it is not make-up that I want: I want to see through her skin, just for a moment.

I move to the dresses swinging off a metal clothes rack— some scarlet, some beaded for the evening, some still wrapped in plastic and smelling acidic from the dry cleaners, others slightly sweaty, telling of some clandestine night in a dance club and their eventual fate, thrown to the floor of some strange bedroom.

I choose a summer frock. I draw it over my head. My penis, still damp from her, sticks slightly against the silk as I pull the fabric down over my body. The dress is tight around the shoulders and only just covers my nakedness. I don't want to look in the mirror. I'm not a cross-dresser. I just want this moment—of being her, of feeling vulnerable in that pliant body. My hands trail up to the empty pockets where her breasts would sit.

Outside the traffic is a distant roar, outside it's a Saturday night. People mill on the pavements in search of escape, a meal, an encounter that takes them out of their skin, out of their marriages, out of their lives. I lie down and fall asleep.

THE BOYFRIEND

Dee. That's what he calls himself. Dee. I like it, it conjures up a certain masculinity I find irresistible. Nothing queeny about this guy—that's what first attracted me to him. He appeared straight, as if his sexuality was a secondary issue in his life. As if he was comfortable with it, and didn't have to flaunt it all over the clubs. He's tall, with a really good body. One of those smooth chests you can just rub your chin down, and a washboard stomach. Not a gym bunny, oh no, this body was built for heavy manual labor. A body that has purpose, that always turns me on. Real muscles, not like those pumped up fluffy numbers. And his cock—you know, a heavy circumcised number with a decent-sized knob at the end. And low-slung balls; I like holding the weight of them in my hand.

It wasn't love. I'd given up on that one! No, it was definitely lust. Uncomplicated, animal and entirely satisfying. Love was the last thing I needed, especially after the previous debacle. Put me in a room and I'm bound to zoom in on the nearest psychopath. I'm in love with trouble. Shrink tells me it's my comfort zone. But Dee wasn't trouble. He was just lovely. Some people are, you know, uncomplicated.

THE LOVER

I met him at La Cage. I go there occasionally. It's just part of my personality. I don't question it. I reckon there's a lot of heartache out there from people living through their head and not their hearts. Me, I just live.

I noticed him straight away—I guess it was his longish ginger hair. Not many men have good hair like that; it made him stand out. He looked a little less fashion-conscious than the rest. I liked that—a bit frayed around the edges, a little vulnerable. I walked up and stood next to him, and ordered a drink. I could feel him checking me out. His eyes running around the edge of my shirt and burrowing in between my legs. I've always liked this moment best. There's never any doubt in my mind that they won't want me. Some people just embody sex, and I'm one of them. I cultivate it. I'm not being arrogant or anything. It's just plain fact. One that's never failed me.

So he turns around, and finally I see his face. Late twenties, aquiline nose, good skin, a full mouth and green eyes, with a heap of irony glittering in there. My kind of boy.

"Simon," he tells me. "Simon. But don't tell me yours. Let's stay strangers for a while at least." And I know I have to have him.

LOOKING FOR STRANGE

They break into a commission flat, an ugly place just behind the club. Dee's heart is thumping, despite a pretense of indifference. He doesn't know this man, but he wants him, and the danger of the situation thrills him as much as it thrills Simon. It is Simon's idea to come here. He does it regularly, he tells Dee casually. You just break in and fuck in the bed. It's wild, and totally alien—plus there's the added thrill of the possibility of being caught. He wets his bottom lip with the tip of his tongue. The gesture is deliberate but slight enough to seem natural. It gives Dee an immediate erection.

Small rooms, damp walls, small town poverty. Simon takes Dee's hand and quickly leads him to the bedroom.

A single futon on the floor, an old cot pushed up against the wall, the wooden bars broken in places.

Simon throws a teddy bear off the bed, and suddenly drops to his knee in front of Dee. Biting the skin around his waist, he unzips the tight jeans. Dee's cock springs out, proud and rudely pink under the naked lightbulb. He looks down and weaves his fingers through a mass of ginger hair, as Simon takes his cock into his mouth, tasting the ridge, then greedily taking it deep into his throat. Dee tilts his head back, luxuriating in the sensation of being sucked, Simon's hands reaching so confidently around his waist and gripping his ass.

There is a poster pinned to the ceiling, an old one of Tom

Cruise. *I'm going to come staring at Tom Cruise,* Dee finds himself thinking, and wrenches himself away. He pulls Simon down onto the bed, tugging off his T-shirt. Tracing the fine down of golden hair around his nipples, he buries his face into Simon's armpit, filling his nostrils with the pungent smell of male sweat: stronger, sweeter—younger than his own. He reaches down and roughly pulls off Simon's beaten leather pants. Simon's cock, smaller than his, rubs against the shaft of his own thick member. A valley of white freckled skin, the testicles covered in sparse golden hair. Dee holds Simon's cock and rubs it gently across his lips and eyelids. It never ceases to amaze him, this similarity of flesh. The same, but different. The knob is slightly wet. He teases him by using it to trace the outline of his lips, his stubble. Simon gasps, and pulls Dee up to his face.

Dee lies with his full body weight resting on Simon. Nipple to nipple, cock to cock. He loses himself in the green of Simon's irises. A clear deep green, freckled with gray. He closes his eyes and feels Simon's lips on his, his tongue entering him like a cock, probing his mouth, his throat. He lifts Simon's legs high over his shoulders. Reaching into his back pocket for a condom, he pins Simon down as he rolls the condom carefully over himself.

"We could get caught any minute," Simon's voice is thick with lust.

"Isn't that what you want?" Dee whispers hoarsely into Simon's ear as he enters him, plunging deep into his taut ass.

THE GIRLFRIEND

We've been lovers for eighteen months now. How would I describe him? Silent, one of those working-class Australians—

you know, not really trained in the art of being emotionally expressive. I guess that's what I liked about him in the first place. His difficulty. His toughness.

Dee works with his hands. You can tell straightaway by the way they hang down, strong, veined.

He's a landscape gardener, works for the council. I'd sometimes see him in the botanical gardens in his dark cotton overalls, on his knees, weeding a flower bed or attending to the herb garden. Then later, at my place, he'd make love to me with the soil still under his fingernails, smelling of eucalyptus.

We met at a dinner party. I didn't mean to fall in love with a landscape gardener. But, as much as I'd like it to be, love is not logical. My colleagues at the law firm think I'm a control freak. I like things to be neat—everything in its place. Dee is my only exception. He refuses to fit anywhere: not into my long-term plans, not into my social activities, not into my definition of what a lover should be. He sets his own terms and I acquiesce. After all, arbitration is my forte. Is this love or masochism?

He took me once, at night in the park. It must have been about 100 degrees, too hot to sleep. We were drunk, the moon was bright. One of those nights, where you have an objectivity about being human, being part of the human race, as if you could stand out there on some nebular body and look back at earth. And then, if you're lucky, you get lifted up and thrown headfirst into the meaning of eternal.

I remember the moonlight falling onto the stone statues as we walked along—magical, blue, casting shadows over granite angels, waxy night jasmine, huge white magnolias curling up in the night, a blue shower of jacaranda petals fluttering down across our hair.

I turn, laughing, to find him gone, completely disappeared into the shadows. Suddenly sober, I call out his name. It returns echoing, the tremor in my voice scaring me. Above me bats chat and cackle. I stumble toward a huge elm, its trunk veined and phallic, soaring stoutly up into the black. I lean against it, momentarily comforted by my own invisibility.

Then I see him, stepping out into the blue-white of the moon. Phantomlike, his pale skin reflecting the light. He walks slowly toward me, his sex swaying heavily. He is nothing of this world, so alien in his beauty. I cannot see his face—the shadows transform him into a stranger. He snaps off a small branch of scrub. Then, with rough primitive gestures, he begins to rub the honeylike sap onto his cock. Around us the cicadas begin their chorus. I am still in my evening dress. He lifts my skirt and rips a hole in my pantyhose. I am naked underneath. The cool night air caresses the lips of my sex. He lifts me up onto the branch of a tree and carefully starts to anoint me with his finger. The sap burns like tiger balm, making my blood rush. He parts me wide open, placing a dab of it onto my clitoris and the heat rises from my center. He steps back, looking like a demented Bacchus, the sap glistening on his body. I am left pinned, my legs spread between two branches, my breasts pulled free. I feel like a sacrificial offering for the moon, watched by a stone audience of goddesses and shadowy trees.

Dee runs his tongue slowly across the inside of my thighs, then bites the flesh gently back down to the knee. I am burning up. I want him inside me. I struggle but he holds me down. I can feel my lips and clit swelling to gigantic proportions, as if my body is centered there and nowhere else. Leaves and twigs tangle up in my hair as I push my hips down toward his mouth, his cock, anything to fill me, to intensify this delicious heat. My head falls back in pleasure, and I open my eyes to an upside-down world, night for day.

Something darts from one shadow to another, an open glade of grass surrounded by a canopy of pungent tropical vines. A statue of Diana the huntress stands in the center of the clearing. At her feet crouches a naked satyr, a beautiful youth of about fourteen. In my drunken, drugged state I see the satyr bury his face between Diana's virginal legs. His hands grip her pale buttocks as his long animal tongue parts her delicate, hairless sex. She drops her quiver of arrows, arching her back like a gymnast. A stone flower turning to a rosy blush.

Hands grasp my breasts and lift me down to the ground. We crouch opposite each other, Dee's eyes black with lust. Wrapping my legs around his hips, I slip onto his cock. Skin on skin, the burning mounts. He feels huge. The moon and the stars dance over my shoulder as I bury my face into his chest. We slip across each other, drenched in sweat, and I can feel each rib of his cock as he slowly pulls out. I throw him down onto the fragrant grass, squatting over him like some primeval fertility goddess. I clench the tip of his cock, teasing him as I move backward and forward, and then plunge down onto the whole length of it. Then together, the moon, the stars, the trees and the flowers all swoop and disappear inside us as we come in unison.

Like I said, Dee wasn't just your average landscape gardener.

THE BOYFRIEND

I lost my virginity to a house burglar. True story. I was house-minding my uncle's mansion in Sandy Bay. It was late, about two in the morning, and I woke to the sound of breaking glass.

By the time I got downstairs he was rifling through the family silver. I was sixteen, dressed only in my pajama bottoms and clutching an old tomahawk, an antique of my uncle's. He was about twenty, dark, tall. He turned around and stared, and then started laughing.

"You going to kill me with *that?*" he asked in a broad Aussie accent. He was the sexiest thing I had ever seen. Afterward I had to beg him to replace the silver but he insisted on taking all the insured items and I insisted that he tie me up.

I've done apartments, houses, houseboats and caravans. I'm addicted to that moment when you first push open the door and you're standing in the dark, the scent of a family, of completely unknown lives all around you, just before you switch on the light.

Ever since then I've found myself seeking out the unfamiliar. Maybe I want to get back to that instance. To be him. The housebreaker in a strange but intimate environment.

THE LOVER

We were running down a back lane. I knew it was close to her house, but I didn't realize just how close. Anyway, I wasn't going to let him know about that side of my life. I like to keep things in separate boxes. You'd never find me planting orchids next to foxgloves.

Next thing I know, Simon's over the fence and into the backyard. He moves like a professional: a quick, silent leg swung over, then a big jump, like a cat. It turns me on, makes me an accomplice.

"Why this place?"

"Because it looks so straight . . . virginal."

Then he puts his fist through the very window I'd fixed only the week before. The light in the kitchen is on. Please be out. Please. The cat rubs itself against my leg.

"Should have guessed you'd have a way with animals."

He grins wryly. I shrug. This time the two satellites are orbiting out. This time my heart is beating so fast I'm frightened it will show in my voice.

He pushes me up the narrow stairs toward the attic bedroom. He's playing rough tonight, short man gets tough. I let him use his weight against my frame as I walk ahead of him, his hands grabbing at my ass.

In the darkness of the room I turn a photo of myself flat against the desk. The scent of her comes up through the sheets as he pushes me down onto the bed and straddles my chest.

"You make me hard just to look at you."

"How hard?"

"This hard." His cock pushes against my lips.

My head floods with images, her hair, his hair, all mixing up as he reaches down and pulls me free. In the dark, this dark I know to be hers. He takes me into his mouth as he pushes down hard into the back of my throat. His fingers plunge into me, and soon there is nothing but this, the pleasure of the moment. He draws me closer and closer and then pulls back, holding me tightly at the base, stopping me. Sweat welds us as we slip across each other's bodies. Somewhere in the distance I hear the click of the front door.

THE GIRLFRIEND

As soon as I opened the front door I felt the draught coming in from the kitchen. The house is small, a worker's cottage from the last century. It was Dee who suggested that we strip the floorboards and convert the attic into a bedroom. I loved those times with him; I'd be in one room, he'd be in the room next to me. I'd be hammering a nail in while, on the other side of the wall, he'd be painting. It was like we could feel each other through the plaster.

I love the size of my house. I can feel its perimeters, it's manageable. I have always felt safe. Until now. Fragments of glass lie scattered across the kitchen floor. There's blood on the edges of the smashed window.

Above me I can hear the creaking of bedsprings. I creep up the stairs, step by step, placing my feet carefully to avoid the loose floorboards.

Groaning. I know that groan, that quick intake of breath. Dee. For one mad second I think that maybe he's broken in to masturbate in my bed. The groaning gets louder. Another voice joins him, male. Something twists inside my body. But I have to look. I have to know.

LOOKING FOR STRANGE

She stands at the end of the bed, her eyes slowly adjusting to the darkness. Dim light falls across two bodies, transforming them into pale ribbons of moving flesh. She holds her breath. It doesn't make sense to her at first. It doesn't seem logical. Her lover lies stretched across the white sheets, his dark skin in stark contrast to the pale, smaller male. Long ginger hair falls across the black tendrils of his groin. She thinks of centaurs. Of war. Of the beauty of the masculine back, glistening with sweat and gripped by hard hands. Angry in its energy. She does not recognize the man on the bed as her lover. She has never seen this passivity, this demure arching of his body as he is entered. She has never even imagined it. But there is a reverberation, an expression her body echoes: to receive. And in that she finds him beautiful, with the blood high in his cheeks, his hair pulled back violently as the smaller man rides him, drives himself further and further into his body.

"Dee?"

His eyes slowly draw focus. Her voice is left hanging between the groans and the sound of flesh hitting flesh.

"Dee?" She lifts her hand and touches his face. The scent on her wrist jolts him back into the present.

"Get out!"

"But I don't want to."

"Who's she? How does she know your name?"

"Get out!" His heart beats unbearably fast as his two worlds collide. He feels Simon pausing, throbbing inside him, so close to the skin.

She steps out of her dress. The shadow of her sex fascinates Simon. He cannot remember the last time a naked woman stood before him.

"Dee?" She leans forward and runs her hand down Simon's back, pausing at the base to push against him in assent. Simon slides back into Dee. She wants to watch. She wants to see Dee's face as he is being taken.

She reaches down to find Dee's cock erect, hanging like fruit as he crouches on all fours with Simon above him. She pushes her sex against Dee's mouth. He finds her clit with his tongue. She swells and traces his nose, his mouth. She has the power now; he services her while being taken on all fours. She watches Simon's cock slide in and out. Each time Dee is taken, his mouth quickens against her cunt.

A translation of pleasure, a medium of sensation.

She wants to be drawn nearer into the triangle. She lowers herself beneath the men, sliding along Dee's sweat-drenched body, trying to find a hold by wrapping her legs around his moving torso. There is something so dangerous about this, her intrusion into this male world. She is both frightened and exhilarated. She pulls Dee's mouth down to hers, kissing him deeply.

He tastes of her, as he takes her tongue deeply into his mouth. His cock nudges gently at the lips of her cunt. She wants him in her. Now. She pulls him down and he thrusts into her. So big, so excited, that for a moment it is like she is with a different man. Dee enters her as Simon enters him. Simon bites the back of Dee's neck as he sucks her tongue deep into him. A circle of penetration. Of give and take. Of fuck me fuck me I'm yours, the feminine and masculine flowing into each other as one receives while the other takes.

She watches as Dee lifts his face. She knows he is close to coming. He grabs her ankles and pushes them high above her shoulders. Simon's small, soft hands, strangers to her, hold her apart, pinning her down as the full weight of both men plunges into her. From above Simon watches her, her raven hair spread across the pillow, her face flushed, her lips swollen and parted. He wants to reach her, this female shadow of Dee, this mirrored love. He touches her breasts, so soft; her nipples harden and grow erect between his fingers. His face buries into Dee's hair, his shoulder. It's almost as if he can feel his own cock in her, gripped tight by Dee's ass. She loves the feel of this strange man's hands touching her, the power of the men combining as one enters her while the other caresses her breasts, her face. Simon's long hair falls across Dee's face, twisting up, entwining with the black, the red and the gold. Close, he pulls back ready for a final thrust. Then in to split, to fill, to burst, as Dee screams his own climax, rushing like a train, rushing like a million spurting gushes into her, feeling him coming, feeling another about to come, her cunt hot, a thousand vibrations shooting down from her nipples to her womb, seeing white, as in heaven, as in to lose oneself in the microcosm of the interior, of cunt, cock and skin, of the distance between female and male as all fuse into one, trembling, as pulsating, a tsunami beginning from out of her heart, from the back of the head ebbing out farther and farther, faster and faster, purple, white, crimson pulsating like a star, like the sea itself, as pinned down, revealed, peeled back in all her glory, she screams out, her cries echoing with them.

THE SHORT MAN IN CRIME

Stacey didn't like to think about her childhood or adolescence. It had been too painful, too traumatic—she was unable to dwell on even the briefest memories. As far as she was concerned, life had begun when she'd met Jock.

Stacey! Stacey! All loopy, large and spacey!

Although she came from a tiny family, she was six foot five in her stockinged feet. Since the age of eight she'd towered over the whole family, having to tolerate the jokes from her father (himself only five foot six) about Stacey, *our resident giantess.* She always felt like some weird genetic throwback, hunching over the dinner table, stooping down to kiss her mother, fixing the basketball net for the local boys, all the time wishing that the growing would miraculously stop.

She even hunted through the vast collection of family photo albums, searching desperately for that one tall relative who had handed on her gene. To no avail—the Müllers came from a long line of German Lutherans. Exile had left its mark in the pinched and shrunken frames of her ancestors. It was an unavoidable fact: Stacey was a freak. Lying there in her tiny attic room, bumping her head on the ceiling every time she sat up suddenly, she felt like the cuckoo egg laid in the wrong nest, gawkily perched over her sparrow parents rushing around frantically finding food to feed their monster chick.

Sitting at the back of the classroom, forever slouching over her desk, she watched in envy as other girls flirted effortlessly with the boys, who only ever seemed to treat her with a brotherly respect for her size. They would offer to arm wrestle with her, or recruit her for the basketball team, but they never acknowledged her femininity. It was agony for Stacey, who had a crippling shyness. She could have compensated by becoming funny or successful academically, but the cruel reality was that there was nothing outstanding about Stacey except her height.

On one particularly anguished day, after her best friend had seduced the boy she'd been secretly fantasizing about for months, she sent away for a restraint to stop growing. She'd found the advertisement in the back of a comic: "The gawkiest in the class? Frightened of never finding a boyfriend you can see eye to eye with? Try McKay's growth restraint. Guaranteed to control unnecessary height. $15 plus postage."

The gadget came in a plain brown box. She rushed up to her bedroom, locked the door and drew the curtains. She carefully tore off the tape, frightened she might break the mysterious equipment that would be her salvation. In the box were two heavy elasticized ankle binders along with a roughly photocopied page of handwritten instructions: "Fasten around each ankle every night for a month. Reduced blood circulation will decrease the flow of growth hormones around the body. No refund available."

She wore the ankle binders for a year, until her mother noticed the bruising. In that time she'd grown an extra four inches, reaching five foot ten at fourteen—with the rest of adolescence still to come. By twenty she was six foot two and still growing, resigned to a cranelike existence bombarded by unwanted views of hidden nests of dandruff, shiny bald patches and toupées. It gave her a definite angle on masculinity, one that made men very nervous.

At dances she took to flirting sitting down. Men would approach her, and Stacey, dreading their moment of realization that she was taller than them—and thus usurping the natural order of things—would remain seated. She'd invite them to sit with her, giving some poor excuse like weak knees. The curious would stay, while she chatted on brightly, a bit too brightly, a bit too incessantly, as the anticipation of standing grew in the pit of her stomach.

Dancing meant that most men would be conversing with her nipples. She would have to hold them at arm's length, terrified that any proximity would look too obscene. Ridicule was her constant terror, from the moment she woke up to the moment she lay down, horizontal and safe in her extra-long single bed. With her long arms wrapped around herself, Stacey would rock herself to sleep, her electric blanket humming beneath her.

She lost her virginity at twenty-seven to a drunken brickie who mistook her for a transvestite hooker. On finally relieving her of her underpants, he voiced his disappointment, but fucked her anyway. It was a grubby and rather uncomfortable affair, but Stacey was glad to be rid of her virginity; at least she didn't have to wear that too, like a stigmata.

She worked behind the counter at a branch of a gambling enterprise collecting money and distributing the betting slips. It was a man's world, but one that was too distracted to notice or dwell on any physical anomaly. She was quiet, efficient and had a knack of talking down the occasional devastated gambler. In another life she could have been a good nurse or social worker, but the scale of her world had been totally distorted by her size. Fear made her innately clumsy and she was forever tipping things over with her huge awkward hands.

Des, her boss, a cheerful man in his late sixties, liked her and was secretly thankful that she was the only employee who never asked for a pay raise and was even grateful to work on public holidays.

She'd walk in every morning in her usual plain blue dress that covered up her ample bosom and remarkably good legs. She matched the dress with a short cardigan, heavy tights and flat shoes. Buying clothes had always been a problem. It was painful negotiating the changing rooms with the stark reflections of herself in the full-length mirrors, some of which cut off her head completely, leaving her torso strangely dismembered in bra and pants. It was terrifying having to ask for a skirt of the right length. She was a size sixteen, not fat but womanly, as her mother kept saying proudly, while wondering where the bosom and height had come from; it certainly wasn't *her* side of the family.

Stacey's uniform brought her invisibility, carefully constructed to make her melt into the very walls. She could stand at the bus stop and not get noticed, sit opposite an attractive man and not blush as she reached up to pull the cord.

It was his height that initially attracted her—five foot one or two at the most. He was a flashy dresser, always in gray, blue or pale-green suits, the padded shoulders of which only seemed to emphasize his lack of height. His shirts were expen-

sive but in atrocious taste, invariably undone to display a virile
growth of chest hair, buried in the center of which shone a
heavy gold chain. A mass of black curly hair worn to his shoulders framed a podgy face of bog Irish ancestry. His eyes were
his most beautiful feature, a piercing blue, shining behind sur-
prisingly long black eyelashes. His age was difficult to deter-
mine, but almost certainly between the mid-thirties and
forties. Stress, and possibly drink, had blurred the features,
which somewhere in his youth might have optimistically been
described as elfin.

Jock was the first man she'd met who acknowledged her
womanliness. He complimented her hair or her complexion,
grabbing her hand as she passed him the betting slip and saying things like, "The deeper the treasure is buried, the greater
the joy in discovery." At first she was terrified he was parody-
ing her, but he was insistent, staring intensely into her eyes,
while his own seemed to convey such warmth and passion that
at times she felt as if he was making love to her right there in
the middle of the TAB.

His authority and the way the other men revered him
excited her. He seemed totally confident in his swaggering and
aggressive presence. It was as if he had used his diminutive
stature as a propellant to power. Soon she found herself dreaming about him at night. She wondered what it would be like to
have that head of long hair buried between her breasts.

It is the day of the Adelaide Cup, one of the grand events of
the Australian racing calendar. Stacey is working a double
shift; it is her fifth hour behind the counter, but she smiles on.

Des brings her a cup of tea. She places it carefully beside her
keyboard. She's always liked Cup Day, the atmosphere being

more charged, more electric than usual. Even the regular punters seem festive, clean-shaven with carnations flashing red in
the odd buttonhole.

"G'day Jock, how's the meat trade?"

"Thriving, mate, thriving." The other men part deferentially
as he makes his way up to her booth. "Gidday gorgeous, a thou
on Gypsy Queen."

She glances at the clock, the race is up in two minutes.
Automatically she prints out the betting slip. This will have to
be the last bet she'll take. A thou. The odds are twenty to one.
He must have some inside information.

"I win and you're mine," he says. As he takes the betting slip
he slides his finger between hers. The gesture is inherently sexual in its meaning. It makes her wet immediately, her sex contracts at his touch, hidden there behind the counter. Stacey
blushes, and tries to cover her confusion by shuffling papers in
some semblance of control. Jock smiles at her. Despite herself
she finds herself smiling back.

The next anxious punter comes up to the window. "I'll bet
what he's betting," he points to Jock, who stands, legs spread
stoutly on the ground, staring up at the TV monitor.

"Sorry, you're too late."

The gates go up and the racing call begins, fast and hard.
The old world of Australian masculinity sweeps Stacey up in a
false sense of security, taking her back to her father's knee on
a Saturday afternoon by the radio. Watching the race on the
video monitor in the corner she finds her heart accelerating,
racing up there with Jock's horse, in the outside lane, limbs
straining, sweat on the flanks, arching forward with each
bound of those lean legs, past the first horse, then the second.
She wants him to win, she wants him to take her like this.

"And it's Yellow Sky fast behind Lovesick close to Gypsy Queen who is lagging way behind in the pack and they're coming up to the fourth lap. Who will take that corner? And it's Gypsy Queen in fourth. She's gaining pace. Look at that filly go! And it's Yellow Sky close on Lovesick in second, hundred and fifty meters to go. Gypsy Queen has just overtaken Yellow Sky in third, neck-to-neck with Lovesick. She's gaining, it's going to be a photo finish . . . and it's Gypsy Queen! What a horse! What a race! Tremendous odds . . ."

A shout goes up among the punters. Jock is screaming at the top of his lungs. "I done it! I bloody done it!"

He runs in behind the counter, grabs her hand and pulls her to her feet. "Fuck, you're tall. I like that. It's sexy. Eh, Des! I'm just borrowing your staff, okay? You won't mind, especially after you've paid me the twenty thou you owe me!"

Des smiles nervously down at this tiny man who dances around Stacey. Jock propels her toward the door, his hand pushing proprietorially against her buttocks.

"I told yer if I won you're mine."

The regulars look on with respect as Jock opens the door of a bright red Mercedes sports parked outside the shop. For once Stacey does not feel ridiculous.

He glances across at her, under the bravado he's nervous. There is something impenetrable about her cool veneer that scares him. It has been a long time since he has wanted a woman this much. But if it scares you, he thinks to himself, it's always worth doing. He wants her to want him for himself, for what he still sees himself as—the short, bullied kid who learned to fight back harder, who learned to use his mind to out-wit his enemies. There is an empathy between them he recognizes, the empathy of being outsiders. Her vulnerability shows in her movements: the way she stoops to try to make herself smaller, the way she hides her large hands in her lap.

"What are you going to do with the money?"

"It's not the money, it's winning. That's what I'm addicted to."

"But you could always lose."

"Risk, Stacey; when faced with the choice, always take the dangerous way. It pays off."

"Well, I've taken a risk now, taking off with you." She smiles cheekily. His interest in her gives her courage. She stretches her legs in the small car, feeling his eyes following her every movement.

"The bigger the risk, the bigger the pay-off." He smiles back. He wants to see those long limbs out of control, to discover all of her beauty. He can scarcely believe that she is sitting in his car, but none of his anticipation shows as he smoothly shifts the car into fifth gear.

He takes her shopping. Striding defiantly beside her into David Jones, and heading straight for the lingerie department, he orders bra, stockings and underpants, guessing her size precisely. He is exacting about the length of the stockings and the quality of the imported Parisian silk teddy he wants to buy. Stacey, totally seduced by the utter confidence of this man who ignores the whispers and giggles of the shop assistants, complies, not silently, not submissively, but with a growing confidence of her own.

"Not the red, it clashes with my blond hair. The mauve is better."

"You're right. Why use a blowtorch when a candle will do? You're gorgeous, you know. A goddess—don't let anyone tell you different, you understand?"

She stands in front of the changing-room mirror, dressed
only in the pale mauve teddy. For a second she doesn't recognize this Botticelli creation, this full-fleshed goddess with
loose, shoulder-length blond hair. He looks down at her feet.

"You need shoes."

In the shoe department he runs through a list of designers
with the shop assistant, whose attitude metamorphoses from
one of ridicule to open respect. Jock knows his designers, from
Charles Jourdan through to Walter Stieger. Stacey, nervous
about volunteering her foot size, remains mute, pinned into a
chair, wishing herself smaller as she tentatively arches forward
one long leg, her foot seeming to stretch out for miles.

"What size, Madam?" She thinks she can detect a hint of
mockery under the tone.

"Twelve," she whispers.

Jock leaps up in excitement as the shop assistant gazes on in
mild astonishment. "Twelve!"

He yells out to the passing trade. "Twelve! What a woman!
What a glorious mass of female flesh!"

Peeved at this emotive display the shop assistant hurries out
the back to locate the appropriate shoe. Jock kneels at Stacey's
feet, running his small muscular hands up the inside of her
calves. His touch sends a shiver of expectation up her legs. He
smiles suddenly, a brilliant, strangely child-like grin, open and
mischievous. "Don't ever be ashamed of your size. It is power,
it is what makes you different from the rest of the plebeians."

He buys her a size-twelve pair of patent leather deep red
Charles Jourdan stilettos. She stands six foot seven in them,
towering over both him and the shop assistant. Jock insists that
she wear the shoes, along with the Chanel suit, Dior stockings
and Guy Laroche teddy, back to the car. The only thing about

her appearance that remains untouched is her hair, which at his order she wears loose and unravelled down her back.

They fly along in the Mercedes. Despite sitting on a cushion, Jock can barely glance over the dashboard. Luckily for Stacey, the car has its top down, so she can stretch her neck back as far as she likes. Hair flying back, the black silk of the Chanel suit fitting snugly across her broad bosom, the length of stockinged leg shimmering expensively beneath her, Stacey feels glamorous.

Jock has one hand on the wheel and the other on her knee, as he talks incessantly about his empire. Meat. More specifically butchers' shops, a whole chain of them across the north-eastern suburbs.

"Me father's business see, but then he was never much of a visionary. Only had the one shop all his life; couldn't see the value in expansion, in providing intimate service, cheap cuts and decent offal at old-fashioned prices. Too much of a tradionalist, was Dad. Believed in staying in yer own class. Well, fuck that! And I did, well and truly. Now I can hobnob with the best. I earn as much as them—what's more I earned it all myself, didn't get some poxy handout from some rich daddy. Nothing's sweeter than money you've earned for yourself, believe me, Stacey. That name doesn't suit you, you know. From now on I'm gonna call you Stance.

"How tall are you, anyway? Six-five?"

"Close enough."

"That's a beautiful height for a woman."

"I never thought so."

"It's a gift to be different, you can use it to your advantage. I learned to."

"How?"

"I knew myself and I knew what I was capable of, and if people were going to dismiss me because of my height, it was going to be at their peril. What it comes down to is self-respect. Look, there are plenty of conventionally beautiful people out there who hate themselves. What is the point? Life is too short. What else are you good at, apart from being tall?"

"Mathematics."

"Good, we can't have you stuck at the TAB all your life, can we?"

She clutches onto her new handbag as they pull sharply into a car park beside a large butcher's shop. The words J. P. MOTHERWELL'S JUICY SHORT CUTS AND OTHER DELICIOUS MEATS flash proudly above the huge front window.

He ushers her into the shop, an immense, old-fashioned hall of refrigerated glass cases. The staff, dressed in long striped aprons and white hats, stand behind each display. There is sawdust on the floor, some areas are stained with blood. The shop is crowded with mid-week buyers pushing ahead to get the bargain of the day.

"Afternoon, Jock!"

"Gidday, Mr. Motherwell."

The staff stand aside as Jock ushers her toward the back of the shop.

"Wait here, I've got business. I'll be back in five."

He leaves her behind a partition. The area is empty except for a wooden crate and a small table. She sits down on the crate and eases her feet out of the stilettos. *I am crazy*, she's thinking, *this man might be a murderer, a sexual pervert, anything*. But she wants him fiercely. All the years of obedience, of being invisible or, worse still, politely ignored, of being categorized as the single one, the spinster in the family, the one who will stay back and help Mum, the one referred to as Poor Stacey. It all bubbles up inside her, like bile rising to the back of her throat. "Fuck them," she says out loud, "fuck them all." It is the first time she has ever used an expletive in her life.

"Shipment due in Iran in two weeks."

"Lamb and some beef . . . of course it's live . . ."

"Bugger customs, what they don't know ain't gonna harm them. Besides, it's trade isn't it?"

"All trade is good for Australia."

Jock's voice and a deep foreign male voice float over the wall. Their tones mix and dip into a low drone. Eventually they break into a foreign language. Stacey wonders vaguely if it's Arabic. The sun filters in from a skylight, flooding down onto her, making her feel drowsy. Drowsy and sexy. She likes the authority in his voice. The power and the anger. There's no hesitancy about Jock. She's never met anyone so confident before. It excites her, inspires her. Besides, it's the first time she's seen anyone get passionate about meat cuts.

She wonders about the size of his penis. Are short men small? She's only ever seen one penis before in her life and that was more felt than seen. She remembers being surprised at how big it was and how soft the skin was.

A door slams behind her, followed by hurried footsteps. Her heartbeat quickens.

"Here, doll, slip this on, you'll need it where we're going."

He holds out a full-length mink coat. On her it reaches to just below her knees. "Present from a furrier mate of mine, for carcasses rendered." He laughs. Taking her hand, he guides her down a pristine white corridor toward a thick metal door, built like the door of a safe.

"The freezer room, my favorite haunt," he says, as a mist of frozen air drifts out of the open door.

"I've got this thing about extremes. Any extreme. They fascinate me—love, hate, tall, short, hot, cold. Anything but mediocrity. I reckon that would be living death."

The light is dim, a soft blue. As her eyes adjust she realizes that the light comes from fluorescent tubes set into the floor. They run down corridors of hung carcasses. Huge sides of frozen cow hang from steel hooks, the smaller sheep carcasses swing opposite. A pig's head looms up out of the dark. She gasps; he laughs.

"I like frightening you. It's a turn on." Again she wonders about the rashness of her actions. Remembering Jock's words she decides that risk is something one must surrender to entirely, like religion.

They reach an open area, where a large wooden chair sits beside a small lamp and a blow heater.

"Sit down." His tone is commanding, authoritative. She sits on the chair.

"Open your coat." She opens the fur as he moves forward, staring intensely into her eyes. He moves so close she can feel his breath on her cheek. He undoes her buttons and slips his cold hands under each breast. Her nipples stiffen as they hit the cool air. Still staring into her eyes, he squeezes each one, hard.

"Beautiful."

A wave sweeps across her body as she feels her sex clench in response. She shuts her eyes, rolling her head back, vulnerable just for a moment. She feels his hot mouth against her neck as he bites gently into the flesh. The contrast between his mouth and the freezing air makes her want him to cover her all over with this moist heat. He takes one breast into his mouth and guides her hand down toward his fly. Terrified of her innate clumsiness she fumbles for a moment at the zipper. He helps her and puts himself in her hands. His cock, compact and thick, dwarfs him even further. It is erect, sprung and proud, transforming him into half-animal, half-man. He leans across and switches the blow heater on. Hot air blows across her exposed skin and up her skirt. He slips his hand under the silk pants and onto her sex, his fingers burrowing deep into her. She moans as he parts her, placing two, three, four fingers into her, forcing her to spread her legs. The tip of his cock is poised to enter her, brushing against the lips of her sex. Her face is freezing, her cunt hot from his fingers.

He strums her clit, making her legs shake with intense pleasure.

"Statistics. Height?"

"Six foot, five inches."

"Bust?"

"Thirty-eight."

"What cup? What cup!?"

"D cup."

"Waist?"

"I don't know."

She is close to coming. The innocent in her cannot believe that a man would know how to pleasure a woman with his hands.

She feels as if she is completely under his power, his relentless fingers, the strength in his broad muscular shoulders, the black hair curling around his nipples.

She leans forward and tastes him, licking the skin of his chest. He smells delicious, feral, musky. The rogue male.

"Waist approximately?"

"Thirty-four."

"Hips?"

"Thirty-eight."

"Shoe size?"

"You know it."

"I want to hear you say it."

He removes his hand and pushes his cock into her, filling her. He is a perfect fit. Skin on skin. A hot ember that spreads up through her freezing limbs.

"Say it!"

"Size twelve."

He groans and thrusts vigorously into her, then pulls back, hovering tantalizingly close to her outer lips, teasing her, before plunging in again. And out. And in, again and again. She wants him deeper. She wants to swallow him up. He pauses for a moment and throws his legs over hers so that he is actually sitting on her. The end of his shaft, now bent, rubs hard against her clitoris. She moans. He buries his hand into her hair, and pulls her head away from him, wanting to watch her come.

"Does that feel good? Does it?"

"Yes."

She drops her legs so that he is clamped between her thighs. He fastens his mouth to her breast and bites sharply. The pain intermingles with the intense pleasure of him moving hard inside her. The faint echo of some Negro spiritual resounds in her head. She thinks she is experiencing a spiritual revelation.

"How good? Say it."

"Good."

"Just good?"

"Ahh . . . ahh!" She screams as her first orgasm ripples through her and the Negro spiritual breaks into a chorus of demented angels, all of them under five foot three.

Somewhere in the vague distance she can feel herself contracting, the echo of her cry still bouncing off the walls of the huge meat freezer.

He smiles, still hard, still wanting more.

"What are your feelings on tripe?"

Before Jock's next major shipment she had packed up her small bedsit with its one-bar heater, poster of Phar Lap, her hardback edition of *Black Beauty*, single narrow bed and dress rack with her four standard outfits. Under a pile of magazines she found the ankle binders, wrapped carefully in plastic. She threw them out, triumphant.

Jock's mock-Palladian mansion was built conveniently close to his main warehouse. The swimming pool was designed in the shape of a lamb chop. She had never seen that much wealth, that much brazen luxury screaming look at me, I'm rich, I've made it!

She tiptoed around the first week, holding her breath, not quite believing that she was part of this lush landscape of thick carpets and quilted antique chairs. Jock teased her, renaming her his great silent Stance. At night in his emperor-sized bed he took to clinging to her like a child, his small torso tucked comfortably between her hips and breasts. She loved this contradiction, this utterly masculine man who was so much smaller than her. She loved looping her long arms around his belly, the fruit of his sex curled up, vulnerable, sheltered in her large hand. The smell of him sleeping made her feel safe for the first time in her life.

At the end of the first week, after a particularly vigorous love making session, she told him in a small voice about the ankle binders. He listened intently while stroking her long flanks, his piercing blue eyes clouding over in empathy.

"It was stretching machines for me. Johnson's height extenders, then the illegal growth hormones. God, did Dad give me a hiding when he found out about those.

" 'Son,' he said. 'It's not how much you've got but what you do with it.' "

He buried his head in her hair and whispered into her ear. "And look at us now, eh? King and Queen." She pulled him closer, wanting to be inside him, wanting a fusion of their two bodies, spirits and hearts.

It was as if her subconscious had been waiting for this opportunity to submit, to relinquish the martyrdom of her earlier years. She knew this was love.

The habits of their lives began to fall in with each other. Every morning Jock would get up at five thirty, work out on his home gym for half an hour, then meditate in the pool, floating on his back with his eyes closed, wearing only a pair of sunglasses while his collection of inflated plastic pigs bobbed up and down around him. Stacey, on hearing the familiar sound of the water filter, would press her face into his pillow, his scent comforting her as she drifted back off to dream until seven. Then she would get up, and check the Dow Jones faxed in by Jock's stockbroker, Deidre.

Deidre had become a great friend, advising Stacey on her dress sense and on how to manage Jock, who was one of Deidre's more challenging clients. Secretly, Deidre was thankful that she had found a way of influencing him. Jock was renowned for playing the stock market as fiercely as he played the horses and he usually lost. Stacey, by contrast, was naturally cautious and Jock had discovered that she had an innate gift when it came to the share market. He arranged for her to leave the TAB and put her in charge of stocktaking at his main branch.

Slowly, as the weeks passed, they both began to open up to each other. As weeks turned into months Jock's vulnerabilities and fears revealed him to her not as a diminutive god but as a fallible equal. The complexity that lay beneath the cocky bravado endeared her further. If anything it was his energy, the essence of his ego, that began to swamp her. She was constantly swept up by his desires, his career. She felt like a planet in orbit. And, although she was falling deeper in love, she began to feel the strength of his personality hijack her own fragile persona, as if he was seeping into her through a process of strange osmosis.

Yet at the same time she was delighted to discover a kind of silent resourcefulness within herself.

Every day Jock would get her to chauffeur him to his main office, preferring to finalize deals on the mobile phone while Stacey, an excellent driver, maneuvered the Mercedes through peak-hour traffic.

"Two thousand sheep, direct to the port of Dubai. You heard me, mate . . . Dubai, Saudi Arabia. Ahmed el Hassam, yeah, that's the bloke."

He started taking her to the society events he engineered invitations to. He was determined to legitimize both his money and his status. They caused quite a sensation: Stacey, tottering along in her high heels, with her quaint old-fashioned English and demure manner, escorted by Jock, over-dressed in pink silk and linen, striding along beside her. When a photo of Jock grinning broadly, his face practically buried in Stacey's cleavage, appeared in the social pages, he was thrilled, and had the photo blown up and sent to all his clients. To him, this was the pinnacle of success and he reveled in it.

He made love to her every night; his sexual energy seemed

linked to his generally hyper state. She noticed that his body temperature was always higher than her own, as if his whole metabolism operated in a different time frame from the world around him. She was secretly frightened that he might burn out one day, stop suddenly and drop like an insect.

His sexual imagination was limitless. He taught her how to clench her muscles so that she could pick him up, even when he was limp, and make him hard inside her. He taught her how to pleasure him with her mouth. He would pry open every orifice, every part of her body with his butcher's hands. He would describe the individual beauty and function of each part as if it were an act of God. She grew to love her own body through his eyes. She began to see the long stretches of white freckled flesh as a genetic luxury, a largesse of opulence. She started to exercise and lost the characteristic stoop she'd used to make herself smaller. With Jock's help she discovered the waisted outfits that accentuated her bosom and hips, exploiting the shape she was born with. Stacey was transformed.

She became responsible for running Jock's social functions, held to promote both his business and public profile. Under her guidance, Motherwell's rapidly became more of a public institution, renowned not only for its meat but also for its benevolence. With Deidre's help she would coordinate the catering, the guest lists, the tip-offs to the local papers and decide which charity would hold the greatest publicity potential. Stacey was careful to exploit Jock's own humble beginnings as a means of transforming the company's image. It worked.

Soon Jock was called on to open sports centers and visit dying children to distribute Motherwell's Christmas hampers. Stacey even organized a Jock Motherwell scholarship for educationally and economically deprived children. That landed Jock a fifteen-minute interview on prime-time television. Sales went up sixty percent overnight. Jock was initially overjoyed, but as Stacey's confidence grew and she became more and more assertive at board meetings, Jock found himself secretly threatened. Behind her back he hired himself a new assistant, then redefined Stacey's position, limiting her duties to stock-taking and social-diary coordinator. Stacey accepted his decision without question, but blamed herself, suffering silently as she searched through her actions to discover what had caused Jock's change of heart.

It happened the day Jock had insisted that she entertain their Arab contact Ahmed el Hassam, who was visiting from Saudi Arabia.

"He's our main man there. Has heaps of cash, brings in over two mil worth of business. So we'd better put on a decent spread. I've organized the caterers; all you've got to do is smile a lot and look like a blond princess. He collects racing horses, so you two have something in common."

It was hot, one of those days when the sun beats mercilessly down on everything. Jock had asked her to take the Mercedes for a service. Before she left the garage she decided to check the glove box. She flicked it open. Something glimmered inside. She pulled a tiny shoe out into the light—a miniature version of her own shiny red shoes. She turned the shoe over slowly. Size four, Charles Jourdan, exactly the same style, only smaller, much smaller. Everything around her receded. All she could hear was the pumping of her own heart, drumming loudly in her ears. The shoe sat in her hand comfortably. In fact, it was smaller than her hand.

"Excuse me, Miss, but we need to put the car on the blocks."
The mechanic's voice dragged her back to reality. She slammed
the door shut, hiding the shoe in her handbag, and hailed a cab
amid a rain of wolf whistles from the building site opposite.

The trip back to the house was a blur. Stacey gazed out at
the passing suburbia, numb. His duplicity burned hard; the
weight of the shoe in her handbag was like a millstone.

Back at the house they had already erected a huge marquee
in the garden. Inside were tables spread with the most extraordinary collection of cold meats, shellfish, salads and dips. In
the center of each was a curious display of long sausages and
meat bones, arranged to look like macabre flowers—Jock's idea
of a joke. Dazed, Stacey checked that the right number of
plates had been laid out.

Tiny, shining, beautiful. She locks the bathroom door
behind her and looks at the shoe. She sniffs along the shimmering patent leather. Jock's distinctive aftershave intermin-
gled with something else—jissom and a heavier perfume? She
wants to slash the shoe, as images of impaling Jock through the
eye with the heel flood up behind her retina. She wants
revenge. She looks at herself. Her external appearance remains
deceptively composed. Grimly she reaches for her lipstick. She
puts on the same Chanel suit Jock bought her that first day and
goes down to welcome the guests, the perfect hostess.

Many of the visitors are there mingling already: the stock
farmers who supply the livestock, bureaucrats from the agri-
cultural department who are unofficially on the payroll, the
odd socialite determined to ingratiate herself with the nouveau
riche. Stacey murmurs greetings and propels them gently in
the direction of the most appropriate circle of chatting people.
Fragments of conversation drift by.

"Jock has really trained her well."

"Lucky to have her. I mean he's not exactly a paragon of virtue himself, is he?"

She floats by, superficially tranquil, as brittle as glass. She hates him for this public humiliation.

At last he arrives, surrounded by his henchmen. They part like worker bees harboring their queen when Jock steps forward to show off his associate from the Middle East.

"Stacey, this is Ahmed el Hassam." She realizes that she is staring directly into the stranger's eyes. Ahmed el Hassam—dark-skinned, high cheekboned, handsome in a gaunt way—is exactly her height.

"Stacey is my partner in crime, aren't yer, doll?" Jock pinches her bottom. She smiles and extends a long cool hand toward Ahmed. He squeezes it warmly.

"At last, a woman I can see eye to eye with," he murmurs in perfect English.

"It's not often that I see eye to eye with anyone." Did I say that? she thought. How can I sound so calm? She smiles back at him. The novelty of feeling equal, of feeling that this man could physically overpower her, intrigues her. It does more than that. Jock steps possessively between them.

"And there's someone else I'd like you to meet, Stacey. June Thistlewaite, meet the great Stance." Stacey freezes as Jock's new assistant, June Thistlewaite, steps forward. She is under five foot with heels, which, according to Stacey's calculations, makes her at least four inches shorter than Jock.

"Hi, Jock's told me so much about you." A saccharine, high-pitched voice, a tiny triangular face, dark eyes and jet-black hair, pretty in a doll-like way, the exact opposite of herself.

Stacey pulls her aside. "What size shoes do you take?"

"Why do you ask?"

In a flash Jock separates the two women. He steers them both to the buffet table, talking all the time about the export business, tax tariffs, how Ahmed has offered to extend their business further into the Arab countries. She knows she is drinking too much, conscious only of the other woman, her natural grace, the dainty way her tiny hands handle the knife and fork.

She can feel the eyes of Ahmed catching her as she stumbles on the dance floor, bending over to pick up the broken heel of her shoe.

"Come, you need to sit down." They walk past Jock holding court over a group of cattle farmers, their loud laughter exploding obediently after each of his jokes.

"You are married?"

"Not yet."

"This is bad. He should marry you. You are worth it."

"How do you know?"

"An instinct."

"The same one you use for choosing horses?"

"Perhaps."

He refuses to be insulted. This excites her further, the champagne rendering her fearless. Behind him she can see June bringing Jock another bottle; there is something intimate about the way she touches his arm. Stacey turns back to Ahmed. Close up he smells of a sweet, musky aftershave and soap, as if under the Italian suit he is as well scrubbed as his English accent.

"Let's go upstairs."

"Pardon?"

"Upstairs. There is a collection of photos of racehorses, the ones Jock owns."

She takes him by the hand and drags him across the dance floor, past the buffet table, past the frantic caterers, past the drunken farmers whirling crazily around them. As they leave the tent she catches a glimpse of Jock staring at her.

Up in Jock's study they stand before a photo of Jock's favorite racehorse, a mare called Prime Cut.

"She has long, slender legs like yourself," says Ahmed, running his hands up under her skirt as if to confirm his theory. His large hands span her easily.

"Good breeding stock, with a strong broad back and firm flanks." She allows herself the luxury of being able to rest her head against a standing man. He squeezes the cheeks of her ass. She can feel his erection.

"I have never made love to a woman my own height."

"Me neither." They both laugh at her statement, at the sudden awkward intensity between strangers. He turns her around suddenly and plunges his tongue into her mouth, tasting the sweetness of her, while slipping a foot between hers, catching her as she falls onto the carpet.

The room is spinning. It is all wrong, as if the decor fits into the irrationality of her act, of surrendering to a man she doesn't love in revenge for her lover's infidelity. She is intoxicated with the smell and feel of him. She resigns herself to his caresses, and throws her head back as he lifts her skirt and buries his mouth into her sex. She moans as he sucks on her—now she is the conqueror, the one being served.

Her hand curls around something under the couch. She realizes she is clutching the twin of the tiny red stiletto. How could he? Here, in the house.

Ahmed emerges from under her skirt, his face flushed, eyes bright, and tears off his shirt, jacket and tie in one motion. His chest is huge, broader than her own, hairless; his coffee-colored skin seems far younger on his body than on his face. Kneeling on the floor, he unzips his trousers and pulls his penis out. He is longer and thinner than Jock. Uncircumcised, something gold glimmers at the tip. She takes him into her hands, his size and weight unfamiliar to her. Close up, she sees that he has a pierced foreskin. A small gold bead sits at the top of his glans.

"What's this for?" she asks, her voice breaking into the moment. He smiles broadly. "Wait and see." He places himself between her lips, then pushes her back suddenly.

His cock seems to pierce the neck of her womb. The pain becomes pleasure as the gold bead rolls over her clit as he enters her again and again. She is close to coming, his shoulders and arms engulfing her as he rides her faster and faster.

Suddenly she hears a muffled cough. Opening her eyes she fleetingly sees Jock ducking behind the couch.

"Look at me! Look at me!" Ahmed's voice is urgent, close to orgasm. Glancing up she gazes for a moment into his eyes. There is nothing there but this act between them. Sex, pure sex. And the knowledge that she is being watched. She wants to show Jock what he risks losing.

She spins on Ahmed's cock and turns with her back to him. He runs his hands down her broad back, parting her firm ass. He watches himself entering her, her wet clenching as he slips in the whole length of himself. He moves back so that the tip rests between her glistening lips. He slips a finger in beside his cock and traces the moisture up to her anus, massages the rim, then pushes a finger in. Stacey gasps, the pleasure is intense as if two centers within her link and throb. She is close to losing control. Ahmed groans and thrusts into her. Reaching around he cups her heavy swinging breasts with his left hand while playing her with his right.

"I'm coming," she moans, loud enough for Jock to hear. Jock peers out from between the gold frame of the legs of the couch.

"I'm coming!"

Jock's head appears in full view, an expression of pain and fascination dances across his features as he watches this huge man, this giant, take his lover.

"Ahhh!" she screams and grasps the shoe, throwing it full pelt at Jock. It hits him on the chest, bounces off and smashes the photo of the filly. Behind her, she hears Ahmed come in a huge resonating shout while Jock picks up the tiny red shoe and stares at it.

DOUBT

The plane trip had been bumpy. No matter how hard he tries, he can never get used to flying; there is something horribly unnatural about defying gravity on such a large scale. Mercifully, no one had recognized him on the plane. Normally he wouldn't have liked that, being a vain man, but after the ignominy of last night, he was thankful for any anonymity he could get.

Karl leaned back in the cab and flexed his hands. They still ached. Old age, you can hide it in the skin but not in the bones. Tropical rainforest flashed past the window, sugarcane fields with workers in straw hats visible where the jungle had been bulldozed flat. He couldn't even remember the name of the country he was in. It was just two concerts, one at the request of the President of this small island, an Oxford graduate and avid fan of Mozart's. He'd been pestering Karl's agent for months trying to schedule a stopover on one of Karl's whirlwind tours. Finally they'd succumbed, and for an extraordinary amount of money Karl was to play the President's own selected concertos. There was to be no public attendance. Just the President and his twelve mistresses as audience. The second concert was for the hotel chain that had sponsored his accommodation. They had converted one of the old colonial palaces into a deluxe resort for the extremely rich. Karl was looking forward to the hotel; having spent most of the last twenty years touring, he'd become addicted to the convenience and transient ambience of hotel rooms. In his mind, they had all evolved into a monoculture of fluffy, clean, white towels, mini bars and spas. As his fame as a conductor had grown, Karl had gradually created a network of brief affairs that now spread over most of the globe. Classical music, like rock music, has its groupies. Musicians always hold an allure, and conductors, well, sometimes Karl wondered whether it wasn't an unconscious reference to masturbation or digital competence. Whenever he'd wanted, they were always there, waiting backstage or in the Green Room, breathless, youthful, eyes glittering, nervous but alive with the thrill of touching fame.

Him. Karl Pope. The famous conductor and pianist. Available in most record stores.

Until Katherine.

The taxi skidded and the cab driver, large and black, shouted blasphemies as a nonchalant goat glanced scornfully at the car and sauntered back to the curb. Karl suddenly felt very sick. The humiliation of last night sat like a cold brick in the base of his stomach. Up until this moment, shock and the distraction of coordinating his departure had mercifully postponed the memory of the extreme ridicule he had been exposed to. Katherine. She had been everything he'd imagined in a partner. Highly intelligent, funny, musical—but, thank God, not professionally so. She was also fifteen years younger and beautiful. The best kind of beauty, worn like an irritating obstacle that got in the way of communication. She worried that people didn't take her seriously because of her appearance, but this was one of the eccentricities that had first attracted him. That and the fact that she was never in awe of him. She didn't even know who he was when they first met. Because of this, Karl always felt she loved him honestly for what he was and who he was. And it had been love, in a way that at fifty-two he'd never experienced before—or perhaps had never recognized.

Love. For him this underpinning chord had always made their lovemaking transporting, not the debauched sexual gymnastics he had been used to (in fact he'd found Katherine to be curiously conservative) but transporting in a spiritual way. All he had to do was to be inside her. United with her. It was the only time in his entire life that he felt safe, connected.

A pain shot across his chest. The crescendo of the concert resounded suddenly in his head, as he saw himself, baton raised, turning around at the sudden sniggering coming from the auditorium. Then, as if in slow motion, in the corner of his eye he saw a flash of naked flesh and long red hair swim past. It was when he was about to bring in the bass that he heard it—the sound of a woman coming clearly audible, clearly recognizable.

Why did she do it? It was extreme attention-seeking behaviour, no doubt. Perhaps she had become tired of his indiscretions. But they had workshopped that, after all he couldn't expect her to accompany him on all of his tours. She was a successful illustrator of children's books, published and acclaimed in her own right. At the time they had seemed so adult, so sensible, discussing rationally the absurdity of monogamy in this day and age. As long as you make me feel loved, I don't mind,

I just don't want to know about it . . . is what she had said, along with making him promise that he'd use condoms faithfully every time. So why this sudden rebellion? This blatant display of sexual marking of territory? Karl felt suddenly old. Doubt about his proficiency as a lover crept in slowly through all the other doubts.

The taxi pulled up to the hotel. It was a huge early nineteenth-century palace, built in colonial British style. The architect had obviously been influenced by the white palaces of the Raj.

Karl, hit by the humidity as he climbed out of the air-conditioned cab, asked the driver to take his bags up to the desk, then leaned against the car, his Panama firmly down on his head. He lit a cigarette. He'd given up a year ago because Katherine had asked him to, but this was his fifth cigarette since last night. A tourist bus pulled up beside him. The various categories of traveler disembarked: the Japanese, mainly middle-aged and nervous; a party of Americans from the Midwest he guessed; a group of extremely beautiful and giggly English schoolgirls; and one lone woman. Australian. Something vulnerable about her persona attracted him.

Early thirties, small with dark hair, her fragility created a grace about her. And she was alone. He carefully projected the more handsome side of his face as she walked past, pulling at her suitcase. She didn't even bother to look at him. This disaffection plunged Karl into a further depression. He wasn't used to being ignored. The cab driver whistled to get his attention, irritating him further. The days of respect for one's customers were definitely on the decline.

The foyer was spacious and cool. Ornate, with high marble ceilings, it had a fernery in the center, around which the building had been designed. His suitcase sat by the desk. The concierge, an extremely handsome young man of mixed blood, was busy chatting flirtatiously with the Australian, her rucksack plonked unceremoniously on top of the desk. Tall, with brown skin and, Karl noted bitterly, unusual green eyes for a mulatto, the concierge said something that made the woman break into laughter.

"Salinity is my field."

"Salinity? You mean you have a problem with rain in Australia?"

"Drought, bad farming . . . rabbits, you name it."

"No problem with rain on this island, everything is very fertile." He extends his consonants in that attractive Caribbean way, pushing himself forward as if to display to the girl his own evident fertility. Karl can't help noticing the lush growth of thick brown hair on the boy's head. With a pang of jealousy he is reminded of his own thinning pate.

"Any chance of some service here?" He hates the sound of his own rudeness but can't help himself.

"I'll just finish with the lady, sir." The concierge hands a key to the Australian. Karl notes his unusually large hands. Probably hung like a horse, Karl muses bitterly, doubting the validity of his own penis size.

"Room seven, it's a lucky number." The concierge hands the keys to her with a broad suggestive smile. She smiles back. Karl thinks it's time to intervene.

"Karl Pope." He leans back, waiting for the usual reaction to his name, hoping that the Australian will turn around, acknowledging his presence, his fame, but she just walks off. Ignorant colonial, he finds himself thinking.

"Ahh, you're the famous piano player who's going to entertain us all . . . welcome." The concierge's charm, Karl notes, extends to men also.

"Room thirty-six, that's the penthouse suite."

The bedroom was magnificent—large with en-suite bathroom, the bed a huge four-poster hung with silk. It was mock antique, elegant but comfortable. Beside the bed sat a small table, along with phone, fax and remote control for the huge video screen sitting opposite. Karl moved over to the small bar fridge and opened it. It was stacked with strawberries and mangoes, his favorite fruit, ones he always requested on tour. For the first time in forty-eight hours he smiles. He lies down on the bed, realizing that the silk doubles as a mosquito net. The sound of children playing in the distance drifts in through the huge bay window, along with splashes from the pool below. Karl closes his eyes for a second, only to be confronted yet again by the sight of Katherine hanging half-naked out of the window of the listening room. Afterward he hadn't even been able to get a rational excuse from her. Not that he'd been that rational himself. How was he meant to react? Sexual betrayal is one thing, but in your own domain? She must have known what the consequences would be. As for his relationship with the orchestra—he knew he wasn't liked anyway, and that was something that really pained him. But the trouble was that the more he tried to be liked, the less successful he was at it. He was a perfectionist, and expected others to achieve the standards he imposed on himself.

How would he ever show his face in the concert hall again? They must have crucified him in the newspapers.

Characteristically, his agent thought that it was a wonderful turn of events. Frankly, she'd said, you're old news. We need a sexy angle like this to spark up some media interest. Conductor betrayed by wife in auditorium—it's perfect. You watch, it's gonna be great box office success.

He pressed the remote. CNN flashed on, images of an earthquake intercut with footage of the minister pleading for more aid flickered silently across the screen. He switched it off, and reached into the small bedside cupboard, pulling out the brochure found in all hotels, the one starting with Swedish masseurs and finishing with high-class escorts. Even on this small island they'd managed to create a flourishing industry judging from the quality of the paper. Most of the prostitutes were black and beautiful. He thumbed through the photos with their accompanying descriptions in German, French and Japanese. The novelty of paying for sex had worn off years ago. Occasionally, when stress had reached an intolerable level, he'd hired women to perform bizarre acts, like sucking him off under the piano while he played a Scriabin sonata. It had been good, but the perfunctory nature of sex without emotion held no charm except physical relief for him. What he craved now was love and Katherine's dry wit to put a perspective on his generally paranoid sense of the world. Katherine. Would they ever make love again?

He reached over and phoned down to the desk. There were no messages for Monsieur Pope. None. *Pas un seul.* What really disturbed him, a fact that kept tugging at a corner of the frozen image of horror, was the extreme youth of the man Katherine had chosen to seduce. Perhaps he was really too old for her. More than anyone, Karl knew the incredible seduction of young skin. He was, after all, the most fascist of aesthetes. He ran his hand across his forehead. There were permanent furrows on his brow. His jawline, once referred to as having the classical edge of an Eastern European prince, was now definitely jowly. And then there was the question of his belly. Although a tennis player, six hours of piano practice a day did not lend itself to exercise. Perhaps if he promised to diet, to spend more time in the one country, to unpack and stay with her for at least two months consecutively. God, he hadn't done that for at least ten years. But love, he realized, wasn't a piece of music you could play over and over again with different interpretations. It actually needed to be improvised as you went along. And God knows he hated jazz. Frankly, he was terrified that he'd arrived at this knowledge far later than most of his peers. Perhaps too late.

Night had fallen and a chorus of crickets had started up, punctuated by the occasional tree frog. He went to the window. It smelled balmy outside. The scent of the sea was just discernible under the scent of frangipani and orange blossom. None of this cheered him up; if anything it fed his melancholia, the nostalgia that lay embedded under the incredible anger of being betrayed. He was too old for this kind of thing. With that thought rising like bile in the back of his throat, he slammed the window shut and went in to have a shower. It was bedtime for Monsieur Pope.

Later, washed and in the blue silk pajamas Katherine had given him for his fifty-second birthday, he pulled back the bedclothes and got into bed. It was too hot for blankets. He contemplated leaving the fan on, but decided that he wouldn't be able to sleep with the noise. He switched the fan off with the remote and lay flat on the bed, the sheet pulled high up over his ears. After a moment his hand crept down to his penis, softly curled against his thigh. Comforting, a friend that had accompanied him over a long, hard journey. When erect it was the most unwrinkled thing about him. Normally he was proud of this fact, and had often used it as a pick-up line. Tonight the thought depressed him. Katherine's young boy must be bigger. He was convinced that was what she had secretly craved. Big, thick cocks. He felt vulnerable and protective of his own now, cradled in his palm. He'd always thought his was of respectable dimensions, a loyal upstanding member. Probably due for long-service leave now, poor thing. Poor neglected thing.

Christ, he wanted her touch. He wanted to feel her lips caressing the base of his cock in that uncontrolled way that made him know that she was near to coming herself. He stiffened. The image of her sucking someone else suddenly loomed up, a jarring note that instantly upset his harmonic modulations. He wilted immediately. He tried to think back over the years, but he couldn't remember anyone complaining about his size, and he'd had over a hundred women. Perhaps he'd shrunk with age. Everything was falling apart anyway. Lately it had been his career. Didn't that other pianist, half his age and very good looking, get a rave review for the very same piece of music he was famous for? Youth always an inch behind him, stealing his limelight, stealing his music, stealing his wife. It was exhausting.

He turns restlessly in his bed, contemplating the sleeping pills he always keeps with him. A light comes on in the room opposite, and for a moment Karl's bedroom becomes a shadow play of mysterious shapes. He sits up on one elbow, peering across. Just visible in the window opposite he can see the Australian getting ready for bed. She stands for a second, her face pushed into the light, just in her bra and pants. She has a good body, he thinks, with legs that remind him of someone's. Not Katherine's, he notes with spite. The light goes off and she is lost in the shadows. Karl watches the spectres on the wall for five minutes then falls asleep. The kind of sleep where all conscious thought goes reeling backward and is sucked into a black vortex into which one discards mortality thankfully. Mr Pope swims thus, dreaming of being tied to a piano stool by gigantic locks of red hair that wrap themselves around him like the blind tentacles of an octopus. For some inexplicable reason the only way he can begin to free himself is through humming, in perfect key, the full score of the concerto he is to play for the island's President. The louder he hums the more the tentacles shrivel up like flaccid penises, shrinking away from him across a bizarre parquet floor. Gradually, he realizes that the humming isn't coming from him, but from outside. Outside the dream, louder and louder it grows until it becomes a kind of roaring.

He woke abruptly, a wave of nausea flooding up through the sleep. The sound was still there, a throaty scream audible through the opposite wall that Karl recognized as the sound of a woman being made violent love to. He turned away from the wall and wrapped a pillow around his head.

It didn't make any difference. The cry was followed by a moan and then a loud growl. Karl switched on the bedroom lamp. The electric clock glowed three A.M. He was furious, he had a concert at two the next afternoon and he was always up for practice at six. He couldn't function on too little sleep. A thud against the wall and then a low groan. It sounded like great sex. Suddenly it felt like everything was conspiring against him, as if the whole world was out there fornicating, while he lay withering in his bed, forgotten, ignored, his last good years going to waste.

Next door the woman starts to moan in a low, husky tone, deep in her throat. She sounds beautiful and black. There is a rasping sound just audible behind her whimpering. She is obviously in intense pleasure. Resigned, Karl lies back onto the bed. The man was evidently going down on her. Probably fantastic with his tongue, no doubt a totally instinctive man who is able to orchestrate the small strokes, the quick bites and gentle sucking perfectly. He must be, Karl reflected mournfully, I've never been able to get that kind of sound from a woman. Her breathing intensifies, now so phenomenonally loud it seems to push out the walls of the bedroom and make them pulsate. She must be huge, he thinks, nearly six foot, with wonderfully large breasts. There's something about excess that has always appealed to Karl's satiated taste buds. When you're with a woman like that, he thinks, it's like you are surrounded by cunt. There is no ambiguity, just sex in all its viscous glory. A sudden scream that is almost a roar makes the hair on his arms stand up. That's not a multiple orgasm, that's a mega one. Why didn't Katherine ever make much sound? Too English, perhaps. But then why was she so loud in the concert hall? Maybe she was faking it the whole time? Maybe that's why she was driven to taking a new lover? I should be able to make a woman cry like that, God knows I've had enough practice. Forty years to be precise.

There's another shout, followed by a series of bumps as if the man is dragging the woman over to the bed, reducing Karl to further despair. How many orgasms can a woman achieve in one night? Frankly, the occasional experience he'd had with a woman capable of multiple orgasms had left him bored and cantankerous as he waited for her to finish. Maybe he just hadn't ever cared enough, been in love enough, to really consider the woman's needs? And now, at the one time in his life when he was sure that it was love, he'd destroyed it through negligence. And judging from the sounds coming from next door, incompetent and inadequate lovemaking.

It was his generation, he reflected dourly. He'd had no role models, and he was too old for the sexual revolution. Fear of pregnancy and, in his case, fear of God, meant that men were completely impaired. His early sexual experiences were a series of clumsy disasters that had left both him and the girls involved sore, raw and disappointed. It wasn't until he was twenty-four that he enjoyed sex without feeling guilty.

Next door the woman came again in a series of low-pitched grunts. *Maestoso*. Perhaps if he waited outside the door tomorrow morning he could corner her lover and get some advice from him? Karl had respect for technique, and considered craftsmen in any field to be masters in their own right. He wasn't above taking lessons.

Lessons. The image of the coachload of English schoolgirls he'd seen earlier appears in his mind. He could have a lesson taught to him by some voluptuous teacher in front of all those young girls. He begins to stiffen. He notes with a certain amount of returning confidence that perhaps he hasn't *really* shrunk with age. And it is thus that Mr. Pope finds himself in the middle of a fantasy involving ten schoolgirls, a thirty-year-old blonde, several leather straps and an old wooden desk.

There he is, waiting outside a large door from the primary school of his youth. The corridor smells of disinfectant and sawdust. Whenever someone accidentally pisses themselves in the classroom that's what the teachers put down on the floor. Why it would feature in an erotic fantasy Karl isn't sure, but there it is, taking him right back to the early fifties. He sits on a low bench wearing nothing but shoes and socks. He knows he has done something naughty and any minute now he is going to be called into the classroom. The groan of the woman next door distorts and shapes itself into the sound of his nickname as a child: Popee! Popee! He stands and realizes that he has a huge erection. There is no way of hiding it. He tries to push it down with his hands, but up it bounces. Gloriously ashamed, he enters the classroom.

The ten schoolgirls are all bent over their books in serious study. None of them looks up as the teacher, a curvaceous blonde in a very tight leather tunic of her own, ushers him across to stand in front of the desk.

"Now girls, time for your biology class."

Ten pairs of eyes look up at him, all staring at his cock. "Lesson one is how to extract as much pleasure from the male organ as is humanly possible."

He hates the stilted way all his characters sound in his fantasies, but blames it on the formality of having English as a second language. The teacher touches the end of his penis with a long wooden cane. It quivers in response. He looks down in embarrassment.

"There are many ways of enjoying the penis: in the vagina, in the mouth, stroked gently across the skin. It is a blunt instrument of torture, a tool of pleasure, one aspect of your lover's sexuality and his reproductive organ." She strokes him very gently. A glistening drop of dew appears at the end. "Now, I want you to line up and feel for yourself." She taps the desk authoritatively with her cane. He jumps up on it like a little boy, lying down flat. She spreads his legs and raises his arms above his head, pulling tightly so that he can feel the blood rise to the surface of his skin. She then ties him down to the desk. All the giggling girls, pretty in their first budding of breasts, their legs long and slender, line up in a neat queue in front of the desk. The first, a tall, pale brunette, steps forward nervously. The teacher takes her hand firmly and places it on his penis. Karl groans, the girl's hesitancy and fear excites him greatly. Outside of the fantasy, the woman next door lets out another huge moan, sending the floorboards vibrating. Slowly, the brunette, her face an exclamation of surprise at the softness of this ugly thing, begins to stroke the velvety head of the monster.

"You can lick it, it won't bite." Shyly, she lowers her head. Karl looks down at the girl's face. Eyes closed, she sticks out her tongue and runs it along the whole length of his throbbing organ. She looks up at the other girls all staring expectantly at her.

"It tastes sweet!" she exclaims. Immediately, the other girls crowd around the desk, running their hands across his skin, burying their soft faces into his shoulders, his hips, his belly. He pulls against his leather restraints. He wants to touch them, to thrust his hands up their short skirts, their starched blouses; instead he is reduced to being their object, their sex slave.

The teacher scolds one of them. She turns the girl around and pulls up her skirt, revealing old-fashioned garter belt and stockings (a relic from Karl's adolescence that he mourned the passing of for many years). The young brunette whimpers as the teacher pushes the others away from his torso and spreads the young girl's buttocks, lowering her onto him so that she is sitting astride his penis with her back to him. Ahhh! The tightness, the juiciness of her as she slowly slides over him. She groans (or is it him? Or the woman next door?). He interrupts the fantasy and mentally plays the concluding three stanzas of Scriabin's Piano Sonata No. 9 to stop himself from coming. A small paperweight rolls off the side table and crashes to the floor as the woman is slammed against the wall next door. Karl closes his eyes and returns to the classroom. Leaning backward the young girl lies down on him, her whimpers turning to moans of pleasure as the teacher starts manipulating her clitoris. Looking down her body and across her breasts, he can just make out the teacher's head as she pulls the girl's lips apart and begins to suck at her as he thrusts into the young girl's tight cunt. All the other girls watch, eyes wide, some of them touching themselves or caressing their girlfriends. Almost collectively, they mount his toes, his fingers, one lowering herself over his face, until his whole perspective is reduced to the sharp smells and soft stickiness of young flesh as it slides across all of his protrusions, nose, cock, fingers, toes. A blinding tightness builds up in the back of his head, rolling as it gathers momentum, drawing pleasure from every pore in his body, fingers of white light drawing up from his anus, his balls, the pit of his stomach. With a shout he comes, ejaculating all over his fingers and the sheets.

Somewhere in the red-brick corridors of the fantasy he can hear the school bell ringing. End of lesson. The ringing gets louder and louder, and as consciousness floods back, becomes the shouting and roaring of the woman next door. She seems to be finally climaxing with the most extraordinary orgasm he's ever heard. Balls aching, cock shriveling, he is jolted back to reality. An impending and now overwhelming sense of inadequacy overtakes him. He feels pathetic, an old man wanking over the prosaic fantasy of schoolgirls. He, Karl Pope, world-famous maestro, reduced to this. He would never be a lover like the man next door. He would never be able to take a woman to those kinds of heights. And Katherine would always turn to the younger man. Never again would he lie curled against her body after hearing that little whimper, the tender clutching at his cock—Katherine's orgasm. The scent of her, familiar, comforting, his and only his. Once upon a time.

He wipes himself with the sheet and gets up. Outside dawn is just visible. Already, the birds have started a frenetic chorus of activity. He glances across at the Australian's window. To his annoyance, he sees the concierge, slim and extremely majestic in his muscularity, climb out of her bed as she catches him with her naked arms, pressing him against her breasts. They look beautiful together, and so vibrant in their youth. Coffee and cream.

Karl notices the weight of his belly slapping against the top of his thighs as he walks into the bathroom. For a moment he contemplates suicide, then the voice of his agent saying "Brilliant career choice, couldn't have happened at a better moment, record sales are phenomenal, pity about the obituary . . ." comes into his mind. Fuck them. They can all go to hell. For a moment he feels better, until he steps on the scale.

Down in the breakfast room he orders fat-reduced yogurt and fruit, rejecting his usual black coffee and croissants. A waiter brings him copies of *The Times*, the *Guardian* and the *Observer*. He postpones the moment of turning the pages and facing what he knows will be the vitriol of the critics, one of them still scarred by a night back in the mid-sixties, when Karl, a younger and more passionate man, had punched him out in a bar in Convent Garden after a particularly malicious assassination of his work. It had taken many lunches and free tickets from his agent to seduce the bastard back into any objectivity.

Karl flicks a grape off the table. He feels terrible. His eyes ache from too little sleep, and the edge of fear still gnaws at his intestines. He badly wants to talk to Katherine. She was always so good the next day, smoothing his fears with a dismissal. "Eunuchs at an orgy, that's all that critics are," she'd say, pointing out his massive popular appeal and record sales for the last ten years. Perhaps he should ring her. Forgive me, darling, all is forgiven. Come back. But he couldn't—he had lost face and that was unforgivable. The schoolgirls filed into the breakfast room, neat, with their school uniforms pressed crisp. As they walked past he tried smiling at an exceptionally beautiful girl, a vivacious brunette, but she was too busy glancing shyly at a handsome black youth serving at the buffet. It was no good. He would have to resign himself to approaching old age and auction off what remained of his sexuality. A middle-aged woman sitting alone at a table opposite him glanced across and smiled at him. He averted his eyes, looking down at the papers, and said a quiet prayer to himself as he turned to the arts pages.

The *Observer* was direct and to the point: MAESTRO UPSTAGED—MARITAL GYMNASTICS MORE ENTERTAINING THAN THE MUSIC. Normally a supporter of his career, the critic, a rather frigid-looking blonde, had run a litany of all of his previous marriages and infamous liaisons, drawing parallels with his career. She insinuated that his renowned virility might be linked with his musical energy and flair, suggesting that perhaps the extreme behavior of his wife—fifteen years his junior, the newspaper noted wryly—could be connected to his own flaccid performance onstage. She also noted that the echoing screams of the climaxing couple had added greatly to the flagging power of the brass section. *The Times* was no better: POPE POOPED AND DUPED. That critic too found the concert lacking

in tempo and clarity, suggesting that Mr. Pope might be more
than a little heavy-handed with the strings—but then what
could you expect from an Eastern European sentimentalist.
Further and much-needed entertainment was provided by Mr.
Pope's young wife, the celebrated illustrator Katherine Pope
née Handsworth. Her agility and stage presence suggested a
potential career in the performing arts . . . Karl could read no
further. As he put down the paper he noticed that his hands
were trembling. This time he felt truly suicidal. He was ruined,
and the one area he had always had extreme confidence in, his
sexual prowess, was now undermined and destroyed by the
cries of that damn woman. There was nowhere to turn. The
middle-aged woman smiled at him again. He'd been recognized. Taking his indifference as a cue, she got up and hurried
across the room.

"Mr. Pope, I love your music, you're my favorite interpreter
of Mozart. That concert in Prague, I can't remember the piece
now, well, it was absolutely wonderful."

He turned to her. "How many orgasms can you achieve in
one night?" The woman looked at him blankly. "Last night in
this hotel the woman next door must have come thirty, forty
times. Now that's virtuosity for you. Against that I am nothing.
Finished. You understand?" Before she had a chance to respond
to his outburst, he left.

At the desk the concierge is humming to himself. Some rap
song about racial equality, Karl notes, no sense of style. There
is a certain smugness about him, the air of the conqueror, the
recently laid, that irritates Karl greatly. "Any messages for me?"
The concierge smiles brightly at him. In his paranoia, Karl's
convinced he detects a gleam of pity in his eyes.

"No, sorry, man. Expecting something from the wife, yes?"

"My agent actually," Karl replies curtly. If there's one thing he abhors, it's being pitied.

"Had a good night?" the concierge inquires.

"No, I was kept up for most of it. The couple next door, they were, well you know . . . and she just couldn't stop screaming, shouting, thumping against the wall . . ."

"Growling?" The concierge has a broad grin on his face by now.

"Now that you mention it, yes, growling. Who were they? I thought I might be able to pick up a few hints from the man. To be able to make a woman sound like that, he has to be something special."

"Oh he is, very special." And with that the concierge bursts into laughter, irritating Karl even further. Is he being made a fool of? He turns angrily away.

"No, no, you misunderstand. Your room, it's next to the President's private zoo."

"Zoo?"

"Yes, man. That was Jezebel and her mate Elijah you heard all night. Them lions, they make a terrible row when they're making babies."

"You mean, that was a lioness I heard?"

"North African and a real beauty."

For the first time in two days Karl Pope starts to feel a little more optimistic.

PEEL

Candy Perkins closes her eyes for a moment as the huge black penis bumps stickily against her face. She is kneeling, her hands chained behind her and her long brown hair artfully arranged to look disheveled. The penis hovers hopefully for a minute, then gently inserts itself between her lips. She sucks enthusiastically, fluttering her eyelids in a parody of ecstasy. She is thinking about what she will cook that night.

Steak with creamy mushroom sauce. Doug, her husband, likes a decent steak—not that it is easy to find one in L.A. not like back home. The penis leaves her mouth, slides its head around both nipples then inserts itself between the cheeks of her ass. This time she hopes they've remembered to use enough lubricant. She is pushed onto the fake leopard-skin rug while two fingers worm themselves into her.

She can see Doug just behind the lights. He is staring at her, his face flushed. He's started to look more like that recently. He looks too excited. It worries her.

"Cut! Goddamn! Wood problem!" Winston, a tall, shy medical student, whose athletic frame and outrageous college fees had landed him in the industry, is having problems maintaining an erection. The make-up assistant wraps a short white robe around Candy while the fluffer attempts to encourage Winston's cock into some semblance of verticality. Candy's bored. The crew, used to temperamental members, light up cigarettes and huddle behind the camera, complaining about the union rates.

Doug checks that the reel is loaded properly, then hurries over to his wife. "You look great, darl, hot, hot, hot!"

"Do we have any mushrooms in the fridge?" she asks, hating to talk about her role on set.

It has only been three years since they left Tocumwal, Australia. "Exotic dancer" is what she'd told her mother, who was sensible enough to bank the checks and ask no questions. After all, Cheryl alias Candy had Doug with her, and Doug, although not the brightest, had the ferocious loyalty of a bulldog. Her Cheryl was going to be all right.

She'd made a couple of films in Canberra, low-budget, shot mainly in disused office space, a makeshift set and the obligatory bed. Her second film, *Gone with the Whip*, had suddenly taken off in America, winning her the title of second best butt in the industry. It was her ticket out. Besides, her American co-star had told her that the money was better and you had some real status. Status is what Candy craved. She was a consummate performer who prided herself on her little tricks, the gestural hallmarks she had built up over the years. It had been Doug that had talked her into it. He had suggested that she audition in the first place. Both of them had been avid watchers of pornography in the early part of their marriage, and Candy had always boasted that she could do better than the pouting, buxom blondes who always looked vaguely bored. And she had.

"OK, let's get this masterpiece under wraps!" the director, a failed documentary maker, announces, waving his arms uselessly in a vain attempt to boost the flagging morale. They saunter back to their positions and Candy leans across the ottoman.

Cock slides gracefully into ass. Cut to close shot of face, sweat on brow, full lips pushed forward, mouth half-open, tongue extending, spreading lips of cunt. Cut to close shot of other woman. Blonde, bigger breasts, shining, impossibly round and plastic, perfect moaning. Volume up. That's it. That's good. Moan louder.

"Are you coming to bed?" Doug is watching videos in the small lounge-room of their condominium. Candy stands in the doorway holding the dirty dinner plates, remnants of the mushroom sauce still clinging to the china. Doug doesn't bother to turn away from the monitor.

"Later," he mutters distractedly. Candy watches herself giving head to the blonde while being fucked by two men—one in the ass, the other vaginally. She remembers that at the time she'd been thinking about the sea. A dream she'd had about watching it dry up around her body. Funny thing was she'd been wearing her wedding dress. She glances across at the poster on the wall. They'd bought it just for a joke, at the last minute at the airport. "Discover the wonders of Tocumwal," it boasts, above an image of a river with a platypus on its banks. Sometimes she misses home. Even the tedium of the one petrol station with the one pool table the kids used to hang out at. That was where she'd first met Doug, playing pool. He'd been on a delivery run for his uncle, from the next town up the highway, and he was handsome. Now she wouldn't have said it was love at first sight, but she had thought so then. Above the condominium the whirling of a patroling helicopter startles her back into the present.

Doug slips off the couch and crawls toward the screen, staring steadily at his wife as the blonde parts the two cheeks to reveal one cock thrust violently into her asshole while the other nudges blindly between her legs. He presses the remote control and replays the image, the sound of Candy's faked orgasm reverberating off the low ceiling.

"You'll wake the neighbors."

He doesn't reply. Candy shrugs, taking the plates into the tiny kitchen and stacking them into the dishwasher. The dishwasher. Her mum had always wanted one, and it had been the first thing Candy had bought with the profits of her first American movie, *Candy Does Randy*. Stupid title, but Randy, a jovial man in his late forties, a veteran of the industry and renowned for his oral skills, had made Candy laugh as he parodied the director, a young film grad, desperate to make an artistic impression.

"Candy, make a killing then get out quick. Don't become like me, a man on the end of a penis. It's a living but it's not a life."

Randy was the first one to introduce her to dictionaries. He used to read them between takes. "To lengthen my vocabulary," he'd say with a wink, then throw words at her like *trajectory* or *munificent*, rolling them around his mouth like lollies. Candy would watch fascinated as, naked, he'd illustrate the rounded vowels with a flick of his hips—his erection bouncing as his hands curved in the air like a demented Indian dancer. It was Randy who got her hooked.

"Mummification."

"Not now love, I'm watching." He doesn't even turn around. Doug had never used words much. For years Candy had projected a whole lexicon onto his grunts. And for years she'd been satisfied with that until now. The word "vilification" looms suddenly in her mind. For the past six months she'd progressed from the office edition of the *Webster's* through to the *Oxford Unabridged*. But she had never succeeded in interesting Doug in even the shortest, most prosaic adjectives. The idea of using her newfound vocabulary excited her. It excited her sexually.

She switches on the dishwasher and listens for a moment to the water rushing down the pipes. Her feet ache from the high heels, her cunt is sore and she misses her mother. The sound of a cracking whip comes from next door. The video must have reached the S & M scene. A naive young countess marries a cruel aristocrat who forces her to commit bizarre sexual acts. Or was it the vampires? Candy can't remember. It had been her fourth or fifth film and, as most of them took only a week to shoot, she'd learned to develop amnesia in post-production. Besides, if she was ever confused she only had to ask Doug. He'd watched every film she'd made at least ten times, which surprised Candy as he'd been on the crew of all of them. Doug Perkins: clapper loader. It was a clause she insisted on in her contracts. But lately . . . salacious, marmoreal, transmogrification . . . She stretches the vowels out with her tongue. Even sounding the words silently makes her horny.

She puts the kettle on and glances back through the door. Doug watches his wife being suspended. She swings gently in her harness, her brown hair cascading down onto the fur rug. A large man in an executioner's hood and bondage harness, his belly bulging over his erect penis, raises his hand and flicks a

small whip across Candy's buttocks. Doug moans without realizing it. Candy sits down on the couch and ruffles his hair.

"Eugenics," she whispers seductively using the lower descent
she usually saves for the films. He moves closer to the screen,
irritated. She tries running her toes down his back. "Inguinal,
synergism, *pianissimo*." Doug doesn't even bother to turn
around. On screen, her breasts bounce as she swings past the
executioner. In the small lounge-room, make-up off and
wrapped up in her favorite dressing gown, Candy tries to
remember the last time they had a conversation. She can't. He
is always watching.

She looks at the back of his head. A short dialogue would be
nice, something like "osculate," "sonorously," "viscosity" would
be just enough to get her off. Followed by a cuddle. She liked
that the best, just being held. Recently she'd really needed it.
She stretches then gets up.

"See you in there."

He grunts and fast-forwards to the climax, where Candy is
being fucked by a man standing on a chair while she sucks off
another. Jissom spurts across her breasts and face. The money
shot.

It is only later, lying alone in the waterbed Doug had bought
at a discount store, that Candy realizes that she can't remember the last time Doug had even kissed her. Let alone made
love to her.

Through the wall she can still hear him groaning to the
sound of her own faked orgasm as Candy does Randy while
meeting the whip. "Serendipity," she whispers to herself and
cradles the pillow, rocking.

The Promiscuity of Bats

There were ten of them in total: five men and five women, busy festive shoppers. All of them had left their purchasing until the last minute—Christmas Eve. Stacey and Deidre were the last to get into the lift—on the sixteenth floor, haberdashery and household appliances. Both were laden with bags. Stacey was carrying two turkeys, four Christmas puddings and a Super-8 video camera for Jock. She glanced around. The elevator was packed, making body contact unavoidable.

She noticed a small blond woman about five months pregnant. Next to her, pressed into a corner, was a tall, disheveled man of about thirty whose dress sense was still trapped in his adolescence. The way he nodded suggested that he was profoundly deaf. Next to him, clutching a roll of canvas, was another man, good looking, with pockmarked skin. Squashed behind him was an elegant woman in her late thirties, dressed in stylish European clothes. Stacey thought she might be a tourist; she was carrying a program advertising a series of concerts at the arts center. There was something smug about her that Stacey decided she didn't like. She was talking to an older woman, a very statuesque blonde in her mid-forties, who handled herself with a great deal of confidence. Next to the elegant woman stood a handsome older man, obviously wealthy, judging from his clothes. He looked European and, from the territorial way he held the woman's hand, Stacey correctly surmised that he was her husband. The large blonde turned to her companion.

"It's bats. There's a whole colony of them on the site. Apparently they have special mating caves scattered all around the city. Just my luck to have one right on site."

"Mating caves?"

"Bats are very promiscuous. I researched it, fascinating stuff. Of course, it varies from species to species. This is just your ordinary fruit bat. But with giant flying foxes, the rutting males fly into a cave full of sleeping females and start to emit loud cries to attract them. They continue to scream and flap their wings until finally they produce a long series of shrill shrieks, and in the middle of that the male suddenly grabs the female, wraps his wings around her and takes her from behind."

"I've had men like that."

"Haven't we all," the pregnant woman chimed in.

The two men behind Stacey broke into laughter. She glanced around. From the look of his soiled, rough hands the taller man was obviously a gardener or workman of some sort. He stood grinning at the handsome man beside him. Stacey tried to guess his neighbor's occupation but couldn't place him; she noticed that he was holding a cardboard carton labeled ICE CREAM CONES—100. What a man like that would do with a hundred ice-cream cones, she couldn't even begin to guess.

"At the height of the rutting season, the cry of a single bat can cause every other male bat to become sexually excited, in a kind of mood transfer, and before you know it, the whole cave turns into a screaming orgy."

"Sounds like a great game of basketball," the ice cream man, Jerome, interjected, grinning wickedly at Dee.

"Or war," Humphrey wryly threw in, surprising the other men in the lift, who had him marked as aloof. Deidre, suffering slightly from claustrophobia, dipped her head in the direction of the sniggering men. Karl looked across. Australian men are so infantile, he thought, and was momentarily thankful for what he perceived as his European sophistication.

"Or just rampaging testosterone in general," said Sandra, the blonde, as she glanced at Deidre. They were about the same age, but Sandra would have categorized Deidre as someone who was in need of sexual liberation—except for the red scarf that peeped out flamboyantly from under her very conservative suit. The facade is not what it seems, Sandra noted correctly. Meanwhile, her friend Katherine was acutely aware of Humphrey, whose intense gaze hadn't left her body since the moment she had entered the elevator. Normally this would have irritated Katherine, but since she had become alienated from her husband, all kinds of curious emotional and sexual liaisons had infiltrated her life. She was convinced that some great spiritual patterning lay underneath these couplings, like a wonderful message. If only she could break the code. She returned Humphrey's gaze, but found that she couldn't continue to look into those eyes without an embarrassing sense of sexual arousal.

Jodie just wanted to sit down. The baby pressed down on her bladder and her feet were aching. Next year Adrian could do the Christmas shopping, she'd be too busy with the child. On the other side of the elevator, Quin was desperately trying to decipher the smiles and the moving lips around him. He liked the look of the tall, older blonde. She reminded him of his ex-lover; he liked mature women and she smelled good. Deafness had sharpened his remaining senses, and he was convinced that he could smell the faint scent of sex under her perfume. He calculated that an encounter must have taken place an hour before. Lunchtime.

And there was something about the middle-aged, well-dressed man that was familiar, as if he was a distant friend Quin had forgotten about. He glanced down at the man's hands; beautifully maintained, they were the hands of a musician. Quin looked back at the face. With a start, he recognized him as Karl Pope. Quin had one of his early recordings on record. Carnegie Hall, 1973. He wished now that he could speak, but he didn't trust his diction, knowing that if he formed words they would sound loud and discordant. He loved this man's work, and basked for a moment in the presence of the famous. He glanced up at the elevator indicator, now traveling between the fifteenth and fourteenth floors. Something had changed in the way the elevator was descending, he had felt it in the floor through his feet. He was highly attuned to vibrations, not just of physical objects but also between people. It had been astonishing to discover that attraction between people could translate into slight dips in air temperature, or a sudden barely discernible acceleration of air movement. For example, there was a palpable concentration of heat between the tall blonde's friend clutching the concert program and the artist in the corner. The elevator suddenly shuddered to a halt.

Stacey looked across at Humphrey, who glanced at Katherine, who in turn peered up at Sandra. Katherine was trying not to panic; there were too many people in the elevator to be comfortable, even if you did find one of them very attractive. Sandra always embodied such a sensible approach to life,

Katherine couldn't imagine her ever getting up to any sexually compromising situation, even when trapped in an enclosed space.

Dee glanced at Jerome's crotch, then looked up at his mouth—blatantly sexual, with heavy lips that seemed to be begging to be corrupted. Dee's hands tightened around the four bottles of champagne he clutched to his chest. In his jacket pocket there were ten tabs of ecstasy tucked away. He looked back at Jerome's mouth.

Jerome was used to being looked at by men and women, and he returned Dee's insolent gaze. Dee didn't look homosexual; there was nothing feminine about his approach, just a sensual curiosity that intrigued Jerome. He liked Dee's hands. The long, worn fingers seemed to suggest that his livelihood was working with the soil. He'd never had a man, but he'd fantasized about it and there was a similarity of physique between them that appealed to the narcissist in him.

Deidre was starting to quake internally. The elevator had been stationary for over a minute and she knew that Mischa was waiting for her down in the car park. She had the result of her blood test in her handbag. She was pregnant at last. She glanced down at her mobile. She could always use that if things got worse. The elevator jolted, descended a couple of feet and then with the screeching of metal came to another halt. Jodie, terrified, grabbed hold of Quin, who steadied her with an embarrassed grin.

"Thanks," she said. He gestured wildly in response, and Jodie realized that he was deaf. Meanwhile, Sandra braced herself against the wall.

"A temporary halt, I hope," she remarked wryly. They waited in silence for another ten seconds; time seemed to

stretch into infinity. Outside it was summer, and many of them
were wearing thin summer dresses or T-shirts under which
body hair was visible. Humphrey could see Katherine's nipples
clearly under the silk shirt, her pale skin luminous against her
red hair. He wanted to make her blush, he wanted to see crimson seep into those cheeks. He wondered about spanking her,
imagining what that flesh would feel like under his palm. He
felt a terrible desire to pull her pants down to the ground, to
publicly humiliate her in front of all these people.

Dee offered Jerome a cigarette, who smiled and took one.

"No smoking," Deidre snapped, her hysteria mounting. If
only the elevator would move! Dee shrugged and Jerome
couldn't help but notice the beauty of his fingers wrapped
around the packet.

The elevator shuddered then dropped several feet in free
fall. For a second everyone held their breath, then almost pal-
pably they exhaled together.

"We're stuck, the elevator's stuck," Humphrey announced
rather unnecessarily.

"Don't be ridiculous." Deidre's voice was tight with tension.
Dee pressed the control button; no response. "Well, how long
do we wait until it's official?" Katherine tried to inject some
humor into the situation.

"Allow me," Humphrey squeezed past her, the soft, pendu-
lous weight of her breasts brushing across his chest sending a
shudder down to his groin.

Please don't get an erection, please, he thought to himself. His
cock, ignoring all rational pleas, rose to the occasion and
butted its head fast against his trousers.

"If I get to the panel in the ceiling, I might be able to reac-
tivate the elevator. I did a stint many years ago as an appren-

tice electrician," he announced to the rest of them, feeling uncommonly manly. Dee offered to give him a leg up and, with the others pressed against the walls of the elevator, they formed a triangle in the center of the floor. Humphrey stood on top of Dee's back to lift off the metal panel in the ceiling. With Humphrey thus elevated, his state of excitement was obvious, and made rather a favorable impression on the women, Katherine in particular, who was partial to the larger male.

Humphrey unscrewed the panel with the help of a key ring, shifted it across and stared at the complex junction of colored wires. None of them seemed to enter and exit at any logical point. He pulled tentatively at a green wire. He had been bluffing. The throbbing attraction he felt for the elegant redhead had temporarily sent him into a delusion of grandeur. He would save them all and, forever thankful, she would sink to her knees and throw her head into his lap, sobbing with gratitude. He peered down; her mouth did seem invitingly close to his crotch. His cock rose another ten centimeters. There was an audible sigh of awe that rippled gently but perceptibly through the female onlookers. Dee, kneeling and staring down at the floor, wondered what all the fuss was about, while Quin noticed a definite change in the air pressure. Humphrey pulled at the wire a little more sharply, and suddenly the elevator was plunged into utter darkness.

The screams and gasps calmed down. Stacey was now beginning to enjoy the drama of the situation. She calmly reached into her large shopping bag for the Christmas candle she'd bought. Holding it up high, she lit it with Jock's lighter, the one he'd bought her for good luck. The pale light illuminated the faces of the trapped shoppers.

"That should do for a while," she announced, looking like an oversized angel of mercy towering above the others, beacon held high, radiating calmness.

"Hello? Hello?" A thin voice with an Indian accent piped up from an intercom speaker set in the wall.

"This is a representative from the general office speaking. I just want to let you folks know that we have everything under control. The technicians are working on restoring power within half an hour. We suggest you relax and try not to panic. We will now play some relaxing music to help you with this task."

The sound of waves crashing and the high sonic booming of whales singing flooded through the elevator. Jodie let go of Quin's elbow and sank to the floor, resigning herself to a long wait. Dee felt quite elated; he'd taken advantage of the black-out and had run his hand across the front of Jerome's trousers. Instead of being pushed away, Jerome had pressed his hand down firmly, and Dee had clearly felt his penis hardening under his touch. They now stood chastely side by side peering nonchalantly into the dark. A plan was forming in Dee's mind. He felt in his pocket—the tabs of ecstasy were still there.

"How about a drink? We might as well make it a party since we're going to be here for another twenty minutes at least," his voice sounded warm and inviting in the candlelight. "I've got some champagne. French, of course."

"Sounds civilized." Sandra needed a drink. There was something about the candle-lit elevator, with the flame reflected a hundred times off the polished steel and the piped music, that was beginning to remind her of the bat caves. They agreed among themselves that champagne would be a good idea. Dei-dre, finally succumbing to the ambience, had begun to find

Karl's presence arousing, being especially partial to European looks and manicured fingernails.

Karl began to hum a libretto from *The Magic Flute*, beautifully and in tune. Quin vaguely picked up the vibrations of the tune and rapped out the rhythm with his knuckles on the glimmering wall.

"Stacey. I work as a marketing director for J. P. Motherwell's Meats."

"Humphrey. I'm an artist."

"Sandra. Architect. Married, at least I was when I got on at the sixteenth floor." Laughter.

"Katherine."

"Wife to me. Karl. Conductor."

Dee silently pulled out the tabs of ecstasy and slipped two tabs into each bottle of champagne.

"He's being too modest. World-famous conductor and pianist."

"Jodie. I'm a beautician and I'm due next April."

"Deidre. I'm a friend of Stacey's and I'm her husband's stockbroker."

"Jerome. I sell ice cream to little kids and their hungry mothers. And you?"

Dee turned and smiled, all four bottles were open, with two tabs of ecstasy dissolving in each. "Me? Landscape gardener and general maverick." He took a swig of champagne and handed a bottle to Sandra, who had produced ten plastic cups with little red Santas printed on the sides.

Jodie spoke for Quin, "And this is . . . I don't know, because he's deaf, but he's awfully sweet."

Katherine turned and rapidly signed to Quin, who replied: Q-U-I-N. Quin. Jodie pronounced his name aloud, the word hanging like shy fruit before the others, who warmed to this smiling, gawky man nodding wildly at them.

Humphrey raised his cup, "I think we should make a toast. To confined spaces and the promiscuity of bats." And they all drank deeply, for the heat had made them thirsty.

Twenty minutes later the elevator still hasn't moved. Katherine is feeling relaxed—very relaxed. She leans against the elevator wall and contemplates taking her clothes off. The air, although warm, is not stale, as a slight breeze drifts down from the open panel in the ceiling. Everyone seems to be in an unusually friendly mood. Katherine puts this down to the psychology of being trapped. She vaguely remembers reading that situations such as this can be powerful bonding experiences. Did the article mention whether it would be a strong aphrodisiac? She turns to Sandra to ask her, only to discover that Quin is massaging Sandra's legs, his long hands deftly working oil into her shapely calves.

"It's the massage oil I bought for Brian. I thought it might be fun to try it," Sandra says, and giggles. Katherine laughs back. It seems perfectly natural that Sandra should let a total stranger massage her legs with her husband's Christmas present. Katherine takes off her silk blouse and sits there in her lace bra. Karl hardly notices. He seems too caught up in describing the inherent sensuality of Mozart to Deidre. A standard seduction trick of his, this would normally have irritated her, but now she is just amused and pleased for him. The image of Deidre with her hair wild in the throes of an orgasm actually seems mildly erotic to Katherine. In fact she is even finding the styrofoam ceiling erotic.

Humphrey sits opposite her in a corner. She can barely make out his eyes, but she can feel them on her flesh, like probing fingers. She likes knowing that he finds her attractive. She runs one hand down her breast, baring a nipple for a second. No one is watching except him, but he doesn't move. She wants him fiercely, wants him to touch her, to show her the cock she'd seen the outline of so clearly before.

Reflected in the metal surface behind Humphrey are Jerome and Dee. They have been avidly talking about the problems of the Chicago Bulls, as if to reassert their masculinity. Dee's hand is on Jerome's thigh and has been traveling further and further afield as he describes in vivid detail the sporting injuries of Michael Jordan. Jerome is erect. Very slowly, almost imperceptibly, Dee unzips the fly and pulls out Jerome's member, the head of it hidden by his palm.

"Great player despite the injuries, you've got to admit," Jerome murmurs with his eyes closed, enjoying Dee's caress. Dee glances around the lift. In the flickering candlelight he can just make out Karl massaging Deidre's breasts, while Quin appears to be masturbating Sandra as she kisses Jodie passionately. Humphrey has his head up Katherine's skirt as she stands spread-eagled against one of the walls, while Stacey, flushed and excited, fumbles with Jock's Super-8 camera.

"Hope that has a light sensor in it," Dee says to her, before dropping his head onto Jerome's crotch and swallowing the whole length of his penis. The piped music shifts slightly to the mating song of the great hump-backed whale; ten versions of the same plaintive set of notes, the hit tune of 1986; ten adaptations by ten lonely male whales who were at the time circling the Atlantic.

The mechanics, working some thirty feet above the lift, notice a sudden lull in the conversation and laughter that has been floating up the elevator shaft.

"Party must be over," mutters one of them.

"Either that or the bonking's started," his mate jokes, preoccupied with the mechanics of the job, both of them resenting a crisis call on Christmas Eve.

Back in the elevator the candle is almost out and the low red emergency light transforms the scene into a Bacchanal orgy of splayed limbs, hair and breasts, all reflected back a thousand times in the silver walls. Deidre had decided an hour ago that the whole experience was a dream. She did in fact feel as if she was functioning in the past tense, which made the outrageousness of her behavior so much more acceptable to herself. She was, at present, crouched on all fours, like the wolf bitch that nursed Romulus and Remus. Karl lay beneath her sucking at her breasts. The strange part was that none of this felt the slightest bit decadent; it just felt incredibly natural. There was nothing in her mind except the extraordinary tingling of pleasure extending down from one nipple directly to her clitoris. Karl sighed and ran his tongue down her belly. Her rich odor excited him greatly, and he thought he might come there and then, his erect cock lying rigid and unattended against his own belly. He rolled his eyes backward and could just make out Katherine. The artist was sucking her off under her skirts.

Humphrey emerged flushed, and slid up her standing figure. He kissed her, pushing her breasts up hard in his large hands. Karl found himself wanting to see Katherine come with this man. It was as if the man's body was an extension of Karl's, as if it were he kissing her deeply with the taste of her sex flavoring both their mouths. Meanwhile, in the center of the floor lay Sandra. She felt architecturally magnificent, as if she had become some wonderfully designed building by Gaudi. Quin was kneeling over her, running his cock up the inside of her thigh and then thrusting in. Her legs were pinned over her shoulders and held by the ankles by Jodie, whose cunt hovered above Sandra's face. Fascinated, Sandra spread the lips of the younger woman's sex—the turf of blond hair over the pubis, the inner lips reddening as Sandra ran a finger around the edge and plunged into the moisture inside. She could see Jodie's thighs quivering in pleasure as she ran her other hand under the buttocks, one finger slipping into the anus, which tightened around her. She pulled the sex to her mouth, surprised by her own mounting excitement, as if this erect clit was her own. Splitting her farther and spreading the outer lips, she could feel Jodie's mounting orgasm under her tongue. Quin watched Sandra's mouth suck and lick the sex of the smaller woman, close to coming himself.

Jerome clutched Dee's hair, pushing him down farther onto his cock. This was different—Dee was rough in the way Jerome liked to be touched. As a man, he knew the pleasure spots to probe and tongue. Dee's ass moved in rhythm with his bobbing head, moving provocatively close to Jerome. He had never fucked a man, but here, in this crimson dream, with the dissembled figures mirrored back, he wanted to be both the taker and the taken. Before him, her legs splayed across a woman's face, her back arched in pleasure, knelt Jodie. She was not thinking of anything except her swollen cunt and the lips that tugged on it. Suddenly, impulsively, Jerome leaned across and kissed her flushed face, thrusting his tongue deep into her sweet mouth. She lifted her arms, whispering "Please, please," and placed his hands over her breasts. Still kissing her, he pulled Dee's face away from his cock and turned him around. Gripping his buttocks hard he plunged into Dee's asshole. Both his tongue and his cock were circled by tight heat.

Stacey was having trouble focusing the video camera. It wasn't so much her lack of technical expertise as much as her mounting excitement at the images of entwined legs, arms and genitals. At such close range they filled the screen in a kind of pornographic montage. There was no choice—she was on fire. She steadied the camera with one hand, while the other slid down into her underpants and wrapped itself around her slippery sex.

The entangled bodies rose and heaved, breathing together, each registering the moans and panting of the person nearest, each infected by the other's excitement. Dee was the first to start; screaming in pleasure he climaxed, waving his arms around wildly. The vibrations of his cry penetrated Quin, whose low groans reached a shrill crescendo as, convulsing wildly, he came in Sandra. Then, like a pack of cards, they all collapsed in orgasm, the women shrieking in unison like a demented flock of rutting bats.

At the pinnacle of the cacophony the elevator shuddered, then dropped into an abrupt free fall. Pleasure became horror, as arms clutched each other, some praying silently while others clung noisily to life screaming as the elevator continued to fall. Finally it came to a sudden jolting halt and, silently, as if deferring to a greater wisdom, the doors slid open, revealing the disheveled orgy to a group of anxiously waiting spouses and friends.